BLOOD ON THE SAND

Diving for the rifle, Marshal Gantry rolled, sat up, and worked the repeater's lever action. A spent shell casing spun away. Stock to shoulder, he took careful aim.

A bullet plucked his trouser leg. He'd survived too many gunfights to panic now.

Cool and steady, he squeezed the trigger. The Winchester kicked. He saw the puff of dust hit Matt's shirt as the bullet punched the oldest Foley brother dead-center.

BOLT

An Adult Western Series by Cort Martin

#10:	BAWDY HOUSE SHOWDOWN	(1176, $2.25)
#11:	THE LAST BORDELLO	(1224, $2.25)
#13:	MONTANA MISTRESS	(1316, $2.25)
#15:	BORDELLO BACKSHOOTER	(1411, $2.25)
#17:	LONE-STAR STUD	(1632, $2.25)
#18:	QUEEN OF HEARTS	(1726, $2.25)
#19:	PALOMINO STUD	(1815, $2.25)
#20:	SIX-GUNS AND SILK	(1866, $2.25)
#21:	DEADLY WITHDRAWAL	(1956, $2.25)
#22:	CLIMAX MOUNTAIN	(2024, $2.25)
#23:	HOOK OR CROOK	(2123, $2.50)
#24:	RAWHIDE JEZEBEL	(2196, $2.50)

TEXAS BLOOD KILL

JASON MANNING

ZEBRA BOOKS
KENSINGTON PUBLISHING CORP.

FOR
my son Nick
Walk tall, talk straight

ZEBRA BOOKS

are published by

Kensington Publishing Corp.
475 Park Avenue South
New York, NY 10016

First printing: November, 1991

Printed in the United States of America

It will have blood, they say;
Blood will have blood.

—WILLIAM SHAKESPEARE
Henry III

Chapter One

She woke with the dawn, as was her custom. As it had been for half a century. The sky was iron gray, the color of the hair she pulled back and bound into a tight bun. Her plain serge dress was brown, like the limbs of the elm trees in the yard, still bare from the recent winter.

She washed her face with water from the blue enamel bowl on the dresser. It was an austere face, long and heavy-jowled, the cheeks mottled and deeply lined. The only softness lay in the eyes, blue as robin eggs. Kind, compassionate eyes, in spite of having seen a lifetime of privation and personal tragedy.

When the cock crowed she was down the hall, tapping insistently on Willie's door. Tapping, tapping, until she heard his sleepy mumbled response, and knew he was awake. She proceeded downstairs to the kitchen. Willie had stocked the iron stove with kindling last night. She got the fire going, put water in the coffeepot, the coffeepot on the stove.

Last night she had placed a yeast cake in warm water and added flour. Now she added more flour to this thick batter. As she kneaded the dough, she heard the boy clomping down the stairs. Knuckling sleep out of his eyes, he shuffled through the kitchen and out the back door, the chicken coop his destination.

He was a good boy, she mused, setting the dough on the stove to allow it to rise again before baking. She sometimes thought of Willie as her own flesh and blood. But he wasn't, really. The war had made many orphans. It had also taken her husband, and one of her sons. War took, and war gave back. War had brought Willie to her. She had gladly taken him under her wing, and never regretted it. With her husband and two sons gone, Willie was all the family she had. Oh, there was still kin back in the Kentucky hills. Kin she had said her good-byes to thirty-odd years ago, when she and her husband had come to Texas, then a Republic just free from Mexican tyranny.

Water was boiling in the coffepot. She ground the Arbuckle and put it in, setting the pot off the heat. The boy returned with a dozen eggs in a small basket. Setting the basket on the table, he turned his attention to the stone fireplace. It was his job every morning to build the hearth fire.

She watched him a moment, thinking how good it was to have someone to do for. Everyone needed somebody. Folks who only did for themselves led empty lives. Most learned this lesson in time to do something about it. Those who didn't, inherited grief. Loneliness and desolation were their only companions during the final years.

My, but Willie had grown! It dismayed her somewhat to see this. Not really a boy anymore. On the verge of manhood. A fine strapping young man. As big as her oldest son had been the day he marched off to die for the Confederacy. Someday Willie would leave her, too. She would not try to hold him. If you wanted to hold on to someone, you had to let them go. Perhaps he would not go far.

She stepped outside. The sun had just appeared above the green shoulders of the wooded hills to the east. A smoky morning haze clung to the fields around the house. Her husband had cleared those fields, had sown them, and harvested the crops, year in and year out. He had nurtured the land, and it had never betrayed him. A fine farmer, a fine husband.

Her eyes strayed to the headstones yonder, encircled by a white picket fence. Only her youngest son rested there. The two stones inscribed with the names of her husband and eldest boy were memorials only. Their mortal remains lay beneath the blood-soaked sod of some distant and long-ago battlefield. Shrugging away the sadness, she lifted her chin and stepped toward the smokehouse.

The sound of a window opening turned her. She shaded her eyes against the lancing sun and looked up at the second story. A young woman leaned out. Her mahogany brown hair was mussed. The brisk cold gave her cheeks a rosy glow. She pulled a pink wrapper embellished with lacy frills closer about her with one hand, waved with the other.

"Hello, Mrs. Malone. What a wonderful morning!"

The widow woman smiled. "Good morning to you, Mrs. Thorn."

The pretty young woman laughed self-consciously.

"Mrs. Thorn. I'm still not used to it. Just call me Laura, please."

"You *better* get used to it," said the man who appeared behind her in the window. He wrapped his arms around her slender waist. "You're a Thorn now, and so you will be until the day you die."

"Joshua!" Laura blushed, tried to pry herself loose from his embrace. "Don't be so . . . so forward in front of Mrs. Malone!"

She did not scold him too harshly, or struggle too earnestly.

"I'm not offended, Mrs. Thorn," said the widow. She glanced again at the headstones. "I can still remember what it was like to be newly wed."

Joshua Thorn pressed his young bride's body against his. "How long before breakfast, Mrs. Malone?"

"Joshua Thorn!" Now Laura was more vigorous in her efforts to escape.

He laughed, released her. Embarrassed, she fled from the window. He leaned out, big hands planted on the sill, grinning down at the widow woman. His hair was a shock of yellow curls. The Thorn trademark, thought Mrs. Malone.

"My apologies, ma'am. I'm a poor guest."

You're a Thorn, thought Hannah Malone. *You can't help being what you are.*

She had nothing against them personally. They weren't gentlemen, of course, by any stretch of the imagination, but then gentlemen were rare in these parts. Joshua Thorn had been east for some years, and was to a degree more civilized than his notorious kin, but the polish was thin. The Thorns were men, period. Worse than some, better than others. Big, brawling, boisterous. Everybody in the Redlands knew about the Thorn clan.

"An apology isn't necessary," she replied. She thought she knew why Joshua was asking about breakfast. It wasn't because he was hungry. At least, not for food. Hannah was a little envious of Laura Thorn. After all these years, she still missed her husband's strong arms around her. But she had never given herself to another man, though on many a cold winter's night she'd considered it. A woman married once and was forever faithful, whether her husband was alive or dead.

She started for the smokehouse. Last November's hog killing had been a good one. The smokehouse still held plenty of salt pork. Some of the side meat had been rubbed with a mixture of black pepper and molasses, then thoroughly smoked with hickory and cut into slabs of bacon. Scraps had been ground into sausage, packed in stone jars and covered with melted lard. Hannah decided she would fry up some sausage cakes. That, with eggs, biscuits, apple butter, and plenty of coffee, ought to do for a vittle hound like Joshua Thorn.

"By the way, Mr. Thorn," she said, turning back once more, a twinkle in her eye. "Breakfast will be ready in half an hour."

"Better plan for a couple more pairs of boots under your table, ma'am."

9

Thorn was shading his eyes, looking out across the fields at the road. The Trammel Trace ran right past the Malone house. This was one reason Hannah had decided to turn her home into a roadhouse after the death of her husband.

Another reason was the proximity of Stewart's Landing, where steamboats plying the Sabine sometimes deposited travelers. Stewart would bring them out to her by wagon, and they would eventually catch the Trammel Trace stage. In this way the Thorns had become her guests.

She looked in the direction of the road, saw two men on foot. The first man was carrying something, but her eyes weren't as sharp as they had once been, and she couldn't identify the burden.

"Can you make them out, Mr. Thorn?"

No answer.

She glanced over her shoulder at the upstairs window. Thorn had vanished.

Looking back across the fields, Hannah frowned. She had a premonition. A pioneer woman knew trouble when she saw it. She'd seen a lot of trouble come down that road in her time. Indian trouble. Carpetbagger trouble. Outlaw trouble. Her eyesight may have failed her, but her instinct for trouble never would.

She went on to the smokehouse, selected a jar of sausage. Emerging, she checked the progress of the two men. Men on foot in this day and age was the first indication that all was not right.

The trace curved east by north to pass in front of the Malone house. As the men made the turn, slanting amber sunlight glanced off the receiver plate

10

of the rifle in the grasp of the second man. It also flashed off the star pinned to his shirt, as a breath of wind kicked his dun-colored longcoat aside.

Now that they were closer, she could make out the object carried by the first man. A saddle. The rig was slung over his shoulder. The man had both hands on the pommel. Then the sunlight reflected off the shackles on the first man's wrists.

Hannah nodded.

She'd been right.

Trouble was coming once more down the Trammel Trace.

Chapter Two

U.S. Marshal Jim Gantry was six-feet-six and a
shade over two hundred pounds. Every ounce was
hard grit. With his height and rangy build, he carried
the weight well, mostly in the chest and shoulders.
His face was broad, square-jawed. A stubborn and
resolute face. His skin was as tough and brown as
whang leather, his hair black as the ace of spades, his
eyes a pale and sun-washed blue. They were quick,
alert, intelligent eyes. Eyes that missed nothing and
had seen everything.

Since dawn the marshal and his prisoner had put
several miles behind them. The tall man with the
ball-pointed star pinned to his shirt looked like he
could walk all day. He could. His entire life had been
a rough row to hoe. Always without this or without
that, until no privation moved him. There had been
no softness in his life, so now there was no softness in
the man.

As the trace left the woods and skirted open field,
Gantry breathed a sigh of relief. The further he could

see, the better he liked it. Born on the open plains, he preferred country where a man could see longer than he could travel in a day's time. He'd spent most of his life in the big sky country. He wasn't used to pine forests rising on all sides. He didn't trust the deep woods. It was like walking through an evergreen canyon with just a strip of sky above, and you couldn't see your enemy until you stepped on him. Then it was too late.

He studied the house ahead with careful attention to detail. The outbuildings, the windows, the lay of the land in general. When the woman appeared on the front porch, he knew she was a widow. The place suffered from the lack of a man's touch. The fields had once been cultivated. The house needed paint. The porch, sagging at the north end, needed shoring.

The prisoner stumbled, cursed, almost fell. He let go of the three-quarter rig, kicked it. Gantry stopped and watched, impassive.

"Pick it up," he said.

Luke Foley stood, bent slightly at the waist, breathing hard. Slate gray eyes, narrow and furtive, now brimming with hate, fastened on Gantry. Thin lips curled into a sneer.

"Carry your own saddle, you sonuvabitch."

"Pick it up."

Gantry's voice was flat, devoid of emotion, barely more than a whisper.

"*My* rig was worth ten times what this old hen-skin is worth. Why the hell did we leave it back there?"

"Because I thought two saddles would be too much of a burden for you."

Foley was narrow-shouldered, rail thin. But

Gantry sensed that he was a tough hombre. Foley was putting on an act. He could carry the saddle many more miles. He had done so for the past hour without complaint. Now that they stood a stone's thrown from the house, with at least one witness, Foley was bucking the tiger. He wanted to make a scene.

Gantry thought he knew why. This was Foley country, and he was the stranger. Worse, he was the law. Luke Foley hoped to stir up sympathy here.

Red Rineholt had warned him. The San Augustine sheriff had given him free advice, the day Gantry had arrived at his office to pick up Foley.

"Heard about you, Gantry. Heard you're mean as hell with the hide off. But you ain't from around these parts. They call this neck of the woods the Redlands. Now maybe you're of the opinion that out west where you hail from is bad country. Maybe you don't think twice about Comanches and pistoleros and such not. But you ain't seen nothing yet. There ain't a meaner piece of real estate on this earth than the Redlands."

"Thanks for the warning."

"It ain't entirely for your sake that I'm telling you this. It's for my own. If you get yourself killed—and I'd say there's a good chance you won't get out of the Redlands alive—then that young curly wolf will come calling on me. That's the way folks do business around here. I do wrong by a Foley, then every man, woman, and half-grown child that's kin to him is obliged to try and put me under."

"You're a good man, sheriff."

14

Rineholt snorted. "Good men don't live long. I figure you might take a few of them with you. That cuts down the odds against me." The badge-toter glowered at Foley. "'Course, I'd have much preferred it had this sidewinder stayed out of my bailiwick. My bad luck he rode in here bold as new brass and tried to hold up Ben Perry's mercantile. Worse luck I was in town at the time, and not down at Griff's Hole fishing for perch."

Foley kicked the saddle again, once more for good measure.

"I ain't your damned mule," he snarled.

"Funny, you *look* like a jackass."

Foley's face turned red as the dirt in the road.

"You think you throw a long shadow, don't you, Mister United States Marshal? High and mighty Marshal Gantry. That shiny badge don't mean nothing around here. It just makes a real handsome target."

"You going to pick up the saddle, boy?"

"Go to hell."

Gantry hit him. Luke didn't see it coming. He didn't even see Gantry move. One second Gantry was standing there, in a casual hipshot way, Henry repeater cradled in his arms. The next, he was driving a rock-hard fist into Luke's defiant sneer.

Foley cakewalked backwards, sat down hard. His head lolled. Blood drooled from his mouth. He spat out a tooth fragment. He looked up slowly. Gantry stood as before.

"You're gonna pay for that," mumbled Luke. "You're gonna die."

"I know. So are you. You're going to hang for shooting that horse trader in Jefferson."

"He tried to pull a fast one on me. So I pulled a faster one on him." Luke's grin was crooked. "You'll never get me to Jefferson, lawman."

"Yes I will. You and my saddle, both."

Gantry stepped in, reached down for a handful of Luke's shirt. Foley grabbed for the Henry. Gantry had been expecting a dumb play like that. He wrenched the repeater out of Luke's grasp, drove the stock into the outlaw's breadbasket. Luke folded with a long, painful wheeze. Gantry gave him a shove. Luke tripped over the saddle and landed on his face.

"You better pick that rig up," advised Gantry. "Otherwise, you might keep falling over it."

Foley rolled over and sat up. He held his hands out, rattled the shackles.

"You're real brave against an unarmed man in irons."

Gantry smiled faintly. He grabbed the shackles and yanked Luke to his feet. Then he pushed Foley again. Once more Foley fell over the saddle.

"You're going to get tired of this a lot sooner than I will," predicted Gantry.

Foley pushed up on hands and knees. Red dust drifted slowly across the road. Perched on the split rail fence running parallel to the trace, a meadowlark sang sweet music.

"Okay," gasped Foley. "Okay, you long bastard. You win. This time. There'll be another."

Gantry didn't bother responding. Luke Foley could have the last word, if it made him feel better.

Foley struggled to his feet. He heaved the rig onto a shoulder, glared at Gantry.

"I'm ready, massuh."

Gantry gestured. "After you."

Foley trudged on up the road. Gantry fell in behind him.

As they reached the elm-shaded yard of the house, Gantry took a closer look at the woman on the porch. Wide-hipped, heavyset. Her dress was plain brown serge. Her hair was the color of iron filings, pulled back sternly in a bun. Her features were deeply lined, austere, honest. The strong, compassionate face of a pioneer woman, sculpted by hardship. She smelled of starch and lye, a good clean smell.

"Howdy," she said.

Rineholt had warned him not to trust anyone he met in the Redlands. A lifetime as a lawman had made Gantry a fine judge of character. He trusted his first impressions, and his instincts told him he could rely on this woman.

"Morning, ma'am."

"Passing through?"

"Depends. Stage come by here?"

She nodded. "Be through later this morning. Won't stop unless I tie a red cloth to that tree yonder. Usually rolls on by, stops at Tenaha, down the road a piece."

"How far a piece?"

"Twelve miles."

Gantry peered down the road.

"If you're looking to buy a horse, you might try the Stewart place west of here."

"What kind of stock?"

17

"Cold-blooded. You won't find a Tennessee Walker in Shelby County, not for sale, if you're picky."

Foley dropped the saddle and sat on it. Gantry kicked him off.

"You can carry it, but you can't sit on it."

Luke looked pitiful for the widow woman's benefit.

"Lady, I'm an innocent man. You seen what all he done to me back yonder? I reckon he'll beat me to death 'fore sundown."

Mrs. Malone looked sternly at Gantry.

"Are you the law?"

Gantry pulled his longcoat aside, enough for her to identify the badge pinned to his shirt.

"U.S. Marshal."

She gave him the once-over, none too impressed, apparently, by his credentials.

"That gives you leave to beat on this young man?"

"This young man's a murderer and a thief, ma'am."

"I ain't neither," protested Foley. "He's got the wrong man. I ain't done nothing. It's a pure case of mistaken identity."

"No, it isn't," said Joshua Thorn, emerging from the house. "That's Luke Foley, ma'am."

"Who are you?" asked Gantry.

"Name's Thorn," said Joshua, as he brought the gun he had been hiding behind his back to bear on Foley.

Luke uttered a strangled cry, and Gantry lunged forward as Thorn pulled the trigger.

Chapter Three

Even as he moved, Gantry knew he wouldn't reach Thorn in time.

He'd been caught off guard, and he was angry at himself. In all his years as a lawman, he had not once lost a prisoner. A man without a home, without a wife or family, his job—and the reputation he had earned for doing that job exceedingly well—was all he had.

So he was mad as a wet hornet when he hit Joshua Thorn. He plowed into the man, using his entire body as a weapon, driving a forearm into Thorn's jaw, the barrel of the Henry into Thorn's chest, slamming a knee into Thorn's groin. He didn't fight according to the Marquis of Queensbury. He fought dirty, to win. He plowed into Thorn and kept moving, hurling Thorn backwards across the porch. Thorn struck the wall hard enough to rattle the windows and his own teeth.

Gantry was blessed with rattler-quick reflexes, but he knew, with a sickening weight in the pit of his stomach, that this time he hadn't been quick enough. The gunshot rang in his ears. One shot—all Thorn had time for. But probably enough. At such close range, how could he have missed?

Thorn was tough, strong. He was hurting, but he had plenty of fight left in him. He pushed back into Gantry, levering away from the wall. Gantry felt the cold hard shape of a gun barrel in his ribs. He swept down with an arm, pushing the pistol aside, leaving himself open to a jab in the face. A punch that would have put most men flat on the ground rocked him backwards a step. He decided he needed to use the Henry or drop it to have both hands free. He dropped it. Thorn put his head down and charged. Both men crashed through the porch railing and fell into the dust of the yard.

Thorn regained his feet first. He didn't have the pistol anymore, and he didn't waste time searching for it. As Gantry came up off the ground, Thorn launched a kick aimed for the lawman's head. Gantry was a veteran of more than a hundred knock-down-drag-outs. He knew every variation on the theme, so he expected the kick. He threw both arms up, trapped Thorn's leg, and twisted. Thorn ate dirt.

A woman cried out. Gantry heard it dimly through a loud ringing in his ears. It wasn't the widow woman, but he didn't have the leisure right now to find out who it was. As he closed in, Thorn kicked him in the knee. Gantry dropped, then rose into a right cross that put him down yet again.

Scrambling to his feet, Gantry ducked under a haymaker and put everything he had into a gut punch. Thorn doubled over. Gantry slammed an arm across the back of Thorn's neck. Thorn collapsed.

Another gunshot spun Gantry around.

The widow woman had his Henry against her shoulder. Smoke curled from the barrel. She was aiming out across the yard, levering another round into the chamber. Sunlight flashed off the ejected casing.

Gantry looked in the direction she was aiming.

Luke Foley was running. He dashed across the road, hurtled the split rail fence on the other side, and waded through the tall amber grass.

"Shoot him," said Gantry.

She cut her eyes at him without moving her body or the rifle.

"Bring him down," snapped Gantry.

She tossed the Henry to him.

He aimed and fired in a heartbeat. Foley somersaulted and disappeared into the grass.

"Warning shots are a waste of ammunition," said Gantry.

The rustle of petticoats turned him. A young woman was kneeling beside Thorn. She wore a blue balmoral skirt and white muslin waist over a chemise. She was very pretty. A milk and honey complexion, hair a mahogany brown cascade of ringlets. Gantry guessed that this was the woman who had cried out.

Thorn's gun lay in the red dirt. It was a Forehand & Wadsworth. A .38 caliber, single action, five shot. An Easterner's gun. At least, Gantry hadn't seen too many like it west of the Mississippi. He scooped it up and snugged it under his belt before going to fetch Luke Foley.

Foley had crawled some twenty feet from the spot where he had been hit, leaving a blood trail. When Gantry found him, he was going into shock. Semiconscious, drenched in a cold sweat, shaking like a cottonwood leaf in high wind. His pants leg was blood-soaked.

Gantry knelt beside Luke, put the Henry down, took off his bandanna, and used it as a tourniquet on Foley's leg to staunch the flow of blood. Then he put Foley on his shoulder, retrieved the Henry, and retraced his steps across the field.

Thorn was sitting up, arms wrapped tightly around his midsection. As Gantry crossed the yard, a boy emerged from the house with a towel and a blue enamel bowl filled with water. The brown-haired woman wet the towel and dabbed gently at Thorn's bruised face.

Gantry rolled the bantamweight Foley onto the ground at the foot of the porch steps.

"I thought you'd be a better shot," said Thorn.

"I do my best to bring 'em back alive. I hit him where I meant to."

"I guess I'm one to talk," muttered Thorn. "I had him dead to rights and missed clean. My brothers always could shoot circles around me."

"God," breathed Gantry. "You mean there are more of you?"

The young woman's eyes shot daggers of ice.

"Joshua has two brothers. And God help you when they find out what you did to him."

"No, Laura," said Thorn. "He was just doing his job." He looked speculatively at the lawman. "Why didn't you just shoot me and be done with it?"

22

"I should have."

Thinking back, Gantry was surprised at himself. Why hadn't he shot Thorn? By all rights he should have. That split-second decision not to was something he was at a loss to explain. Possibly it had something to do with his low opinion of Luke Foley.

"Why, Joshua?" asked Laura. "Why did you try to shoot that man?"

Thorn wore a sheepish expression.

"Because he's a Foley."

"What do you mean?"

"I should have told you about it before, dear. But I . . . I was afraid you wouldn't understand."

"Understand? I *don't* understand. You're an attorney, Joshua. You're supposed to uphold the law. Believe in it. And here you are trying to shoot a man down in cold blood. An unarmed man. What is it that I am supposed to understand?"

Thorn blushed furiously. "Don't ride me like this, Laura." He clearly did not wish to pursue the subject in the presence of strangers.

"You say you try to bring your prisoners back alive," said Mrs. Malone crisply, addressing Gantry. "If this man is left untended, he will bleed to death. I suggest you bring him inside."

Gantry gathered up a handful of Foley's shirt and dragged the wounded man onto the porch, into the shade.

"This'll do. All I'll need is a hot knife and a bottle of whiskey, if you have it. If not, I can use gunpowder. The bullet went clean through."

Mrs. Malone was provoked by the cavalier manner in which Gantry treated the injured man.

23

"Marshal, I'll thank you to behave in a more civilized fashion while under my roof. Luke Foley or not, this man deserves to be properly looked after."

"Yes, ma'am."

She turned to the boy. "Willie, bring hot water and bandaging. Lay a knife in the fire."

The boy was staring at Foley, eyes wide as saucers.

"That's Luke Foley? *The* Luke Foley?"

"Willie!"

"*Wow!*" The boy dashed into the house. Once inside, he cut loose a rebel yell.

Gantry shook his head. Looked to him like Willie had a bad case of misplaced hero worship.

Thorn was on his feet now. Gantry braced for more trouble.

"You going to give me back my gun, Marshal?"

"Depends."

Thorn squared his shoulders. "Old habits die hard. I thought I'd put it all behind me. The fear, the hate, all of it, when I went East to law school. Maybe coming back was a mistake." He scanned the pine-blanketed hills.

"Put all what behind you?"

Thorn's smile had a bitter twist.

"The blood feud, Marshal. An old tradition. It's been that way between the Thorns and the Foleys since before I was born."

Chapter Four

"It started back in '40," said Joshua Thorn. "Heard of the Shelby County War, Marshal?"

Gantry nodded.

He sat across the dining room table from Thorn and his wife. Mrs. Malone sat at one end. The breakfast of eggs, sausage, and biscuits had been finished, the plates cleared away by the widow woman and Willie. Gantry had polished off three helpings, quick as a plague of grasshoppers could strip a cornfield. He could go a long way for a long time without food—proven it on many occasions. But when vittles were made available, he could eat like a team of horses.

Coffee had been served. It was just the way Gantry liked it. Piping hot and strong enough to float a horseshoe.

"Frank Foley thought he could get away with stealing land," continued Thorn. "He had the judge in his back pocket. The Foley's still do, by the way. Frank's dead. His wife runs the family now. She's twice as mean as Frank ever was."

"Luke Foley will stand trial in Jefferson," said Gantry. "A federal judge will preside."

He glanced across the room at Foley. Luke was sitting on the floor in a corner, shackled to the leg of a heavy oak hutch.

Mrs. Malone had argued that Luke needed bed rest, but Gantry would have none of it. He wasn't going to let Foley out of his sight. The leg wound had been cleaned, cauterized, and dressed. Luke was conscious, white as a sheet. He looked more than a little peaked.

"When Frank Foley failed to take property rightfully belonging to a Joseph Goodbread by so-called legal means, he hired a bandit named Jackson to murder Goodbread. Jackson got the job done. Goodbread was sitting on a hitching post in Shelbyville—unarmed and minding his own business—when Jackson rode up and killed him in cold blood.

"After that, Foley and Jackson formed the Regulators. They pretended to be after horse thieves and cattle rustlers. In fact, they were the ones doing all the thieving themselves. Anybody stood up to them, they started shooting.

"My uncle was killed, his home burned, his stock run off. That's when my father declared war on the Foleys and the Regulators. He helped form a group called the Moderators. They set out to uphold law and order. The Shelby County War heated up fast, and it went on for four years. Finally, Sam Houston sent troops in to put a stop to it."

"That was a long time ago," said Laura. "It doesn't explain why you tried to kill this man."

"The war may be over," said Gantry, "but the blood feud never is."

Thorn nodded, staring moodily into his coffee cup.

"A lot of Thorns and a lot of Foleys lost their lives in the Shelby County War," he said. "There's been bad blood between us ever since."

"Why can't you just forgive and forget?" asked Laura. It was clear to Gantry that she had been severely shaken by Thorn's attempt to shoot Luke Foley. She hadn't realized, never dreamed, that her new husband was capable of such violence, and she was having trouble coming to terms with it.

Thorn gave her a funny look. "Forgive? Forget?" He sounded like he didn't know what the words meant.

"Yes. Forgiveness. A basic Christian tenet. Perhaps you've heard of it."

"My folks come from Tennessee mountain stock. So do the Foleys. I guess you could say the Old Testament still applies. An eye for an eye. Blood for blood. It's always been so."

"You can't possibly believe in that," said Laura.

"It's hard to reconcile with what I learned in law school," admitted Thorn. He glanced at Gantry. "There is more than one kind of law, though."

"No, there isn't," said Gantry. "There's only one law. The law I'm sworn to uphold."

"Your kind of law doesn't count for much in the Redlands."

"As long as I'm here, it does."

"That won't be for long," mumbled Luke Foley, from his corner.

Thorn sat back in his chair and put his hands flat on the table, fingers splayed.

"Know why I went East to law school, Marshal?"

"Can't say I do."

"Because I wondered if there might be some other way to solve this problem between my family and the Foleys. Some way besides guns and knives. I came to believe I'd actually found a better way. Until I saw Luke Foley coming down the road. Then all I could think about was my father. I remembered watching him die. I was just a boy when it happened. He was out in the field one morning, plowing. One of the Daggetts, kin to the Foleys, killed him with a long shot from a clump of trees down by the creek. I ran out to my father, knelt there with his head in my lap . . . and watched him die."

"What happened to this Daggett feller?"

"My oldest brother, Logan, tracked him down and done for him."

"You should've gone to the law."

Thorn snorted. "Law? What law? You wouldn't by any chance mean the Tenaha sheriff, would you? Linus Hoag is kin to the Foleys, too. You think he would have pushed away from the bar long enough to track the man who killed my father? Obviously you don't know how things work around here, Marshal. Hoag would have proposed a toast to the Daggetts."

"I know this much. You take the law into your own hands, you're a criminal in my book."

Thorn clenched his big hands into fists. "I'm telling you that here in the Redlands, that's the only way sometimes to see justice done."

"Times are changing," said Hannah Malone. "It isn't that I don't understand, Mr. Thorn. Believe me, I do. I've lived here most of my life. But if this bloodshed is ever going to end, we must put faith in the law. You of all people are bound to know that, deep in your heart. Why else would you have devoted the past few years of your life to the study of law?"

Thorn shook his head. Here, mused Gantry, was one very confused young man.

"Hey, Marshal," said Foley. "You're so big on the law, why ain't you arrested this sonuvabitch for trying to ventilate me?"

"You watch your mouth around my wife," growled Thorn.

"Yeah, you talk plenty tough when you've got the upper hand," jeered Foley. "Why don't you turn me loose and give me a gun and we'll settle this the right way. Man to man."

"Shut up, Foley," said Gantry.

Thorn peered blankly at the lawman.

"Part of me wants to do just that."

"Don't try it."

"If I don't, it won't be because you say not to."

Laura stood up quickly.

"Joshua, you sound just like *him*," she declared, pointing at Foley.

"Laura . . ."

She turned on her heel and left the room.

"Nice-lookin' filly you got there," said Foley. "Entirely too much woman for a Thorn."

Joshua jumped up, overturning his chair. Gantry got up, too. Their guns were in the adjoining hall. The boardinghouse rule was no weapons at the table.

29

Out of respect for the widow woman, he had abided by that rule. Now he was glad she'd made it. Looked to him as though Thorn would have put a bullet into Foley, if he'd had a pistol.

"Count yourself lucky," Thorn told Luke. He was breathing high and fast. His eyes glittered with a deep, consuming hatred. Reason and emotion battled for control of Joshua Thorn, and it appeared that reason was getting its butt kicked.

"You do the same," Gantry advised Thorn. "I cut you some slack the first time. Next time, I won't."

Thorn headed for the door. He paused, looked back, and laughed, a short and bitter sound.

"That's the thing about the law I can't stomach," he said. "It protects animals like *that*."

He gave Luke Foley a final menacing glance, then left the room.

Chapter Five

Hannah Malone came out onto the front porch to find Gantry's long frame sprawled in a rocking chair. The Henry repeater lay across the arms of the rocker. Gantry was building a smoke with deft fingers, using wheatstraw paper and Lone Jack tobacco.

Luke Foley sat with his back against the porch railing. He was shackled to one of the rails.

"Give me a smoke," said Luke.

"You can smoke when you get to Hell."

Gantry had dragged him from the dining room, down the hall, and out through the front door like Foley was a sack of oats. The widow woman did not much care for the Foleys, but neither did she like to see a wounded man treated with such brutal indifference. She decided she didn't particularly like Marshal Gantry. Not that her disapproval meant doodlysquat to him. Gantry struck her as a man who didn't give half a hoot for the opinions of others.

He looked up at her now, a sidelong glance.

"Reckon the stage got held up?"

She realized he was joking, in a cynical way that suited him.

"In the Redlands that would come as no surprise. A few years back, a stage making the twenty-mile run between San Augustine and Nacogdoches was held up three different times on the same day."

Gantry gave the piney hills a slow scan.

"Good outlaw country."

She nodded. "Hard to track a man through these woods. Not to mention the cypress swamps."

It was his turn to nod. "So I've noticed."

"What happened to your horses?"

Gantry smiled ruefully. "Horse thieves. Last night while we were in camp." He pointed at Luke with his chin. "Thanks to this extra baggage, I couldn't go after them. If you want to know the truth, I didn't even hear them coming. Much less going."

"A whole army can move through these woods without making a sound or leaving sign. It's that nice thick carpet of pine needles."

"Some lawman," scoffed Foley. "His own horse stole right out from under him."

"Probably some of your kin," remarked Gantry.

"If so, they'd have cut you from ear to ear."

Gantry scratched a match on his boot heel and lit the cigarette. He didn't look worried.

"It'll happen," goaded Luke. "My family won't never let you take me to Jefferson. You'll live just long enough to be sorry you ever knew me."

"I'm already sorry."

"The stage will come," said Mrs. Malone. "It isn't what you'd call regular." She glanced at the red cloth tied to one of the elms near the trace, and hoped the

32

stage would arrive soon. She wanted to be rid of Gantry and his prisoner.

She knew Luke was right. The rest of the Foley clan *would* be out to kill Gantry. If they showed up here, no telling what else they might do. They would certainly kill Joshua Thorn. Probably Laura, too. They might put the house to the torch, just for laughs. She had heard plenty of scare stories about the Foleys, and while she could pay lip service to law and order, she didn't want to get caught in the middle.

Turning back into the house, she saw Joshua Thorn descending the stairs, wearing a suit of blue broadcloth and toting a couple of valises. He set the bags down just inside the front door.

"No sign of the stage, Mrs. Malone?"

"Mr. Thorn, I wish you wouldn't take the stage into Tenaha."

"Why not?"

"There may be trouble."

"I'm not in the habit of shying away from trouble."

"For Laura's sake."

"I appreciate your concern, ma'am, but I think it's time I got home." He threw a quick look up the staircase. "Anyway, the honeymoon seems to be over."

"I'll have Willie take you into town in the spring wagon. You can go the long way around to Tenaha, avoiding the stage route."

Thorn scowled. "The long way around?" His voice had a sharp edge. "I don't think so."

Stubborn pride, thought the widow woman, exasperated. Why were men so full of it?

"Where's Gantry?" he asked.

"On the porch."

"I'd better have a word with him."

Thorn stepped out. Gantry was rocking slightly, smoking, ceaselessly scanning the fields and the hills beyond. He looked relaxed, but Thorn sensed the violence coiled just beneath the surface. A bitter core of anger slow-burned in the marshal.

"Mrs. Malone says there may be trouble on the road to Tenaha," he said. "A woman's intuition."

"May be." Gantry sounded like he could care less.

"I plan to be on that stage. My wife and I."

"I don't think so. I'm commandeering the stage to transport my prisoner. No passengers. If there are any on it now, they'll have to get off here and make other arrangements."

"That's pretty high-handed."

"The way it's going to be."

"Just because you say so?" Thorn felt his quick anger surging to high tide.

Gantry didn't move. Emotionless, he watched Thorn. Joshua knew that the violence in the man was coiling even tighter. He tried to control his temper. He'd been taught to employ logic in the presenting of his case, and he thought it was about time he used what he had spent so much time learning.

"I've been East for several years, Marshal. But don't let that fool you. I was born and bred out here, in this gallop-and-gunshot country. If the Foleys try to spring Luke, you'll welcome my help."

"Thanks for the offer. But the answer's no."

34

Thorn's head dipped a notch, lips thinning.

"This is a free country, dammit. You can't tell me what to do."

Gantry rocked forward, rose in a quick smooth motion. The Henry dangled in his right hand. The cigarette dangled from his lips. Thorn braced himself.

"Your wife. She's from back East, right?"

"Why, yes. What's that got—"

"Personally, I don't care if you get your fool head blown off. But I'm not going to let you put the young lady in danger."

"My wife's welfare is my concern. Not yours."

"Then you need to start looking out for her."

"You need to stop telling me what to do. The fact is, until the Foleys are all behind bars, or six feet under—every last one of them—my wife isn't safe anywhere. For the simple reason that she's now a Thorn. So you see, I've a vested interest in having this coyote brought to justice. I may not be as good with a gun as my brothers, but some help is better than none at all."

Gantry picked the cigarette out of his teeth, dropped it, ground it under his heel. He heard, faintly, a distant drumroll. Horses on the run. Turning, he saw the stage appear where the red road broke free of the tall dark woods.

"Let 'em come along, Marshal," sneered Foley. "I'm gonna get my hands on that little filly of his sooner or later. This saves me the trouble of havin' to hunt her down."

Gantry gave him a long look. Then he pulled Thorn's pistol from his belt and returned it to its rightful owner.

"All right," he said. "You can come along."

Luke Foley had a sudden change of heart, having failed to anticipate such an unlikely development. "Wait," he said. "You can't do that. He'll try to kill me."

"Not as long as I'm alive, he won't." Gantry smiled. "You might say I'm the only thing standing between you and a bullet."

Foley turned a shade whiter.

"You better hope he stays alive, Luke," said Thorn. "Because if he doesn't, you might not either."

Chapter Six

The stage was a mud wagon, a smaller and lighter version of the Concord coach, pulled by a team of four horses. The canvas sides were rolled up, and Gantry could tell from a distance that there weren't any passengers.

"Whadya mean, *commandeer* the stage?" asked the reinsman, truculent.

"I mean I'm going to transport my prisoner on your stage. There might be trouble along the way. So I'd advise you to stay here."

The driver was a burly character with a thick black beard stained by yellow tobacco juice. He peered around Gantry at Foley. Luke was still ironed to the porch rail.

"Who in blazes is that, anyroad?"

"Luke Foley."

"Foley, huh?" The jehu chewed vigorously on his quid. "And you're a United States Marshal," he murmured, squinting at Gantry's badge. "Never seen a United States Marshal in these parts."

"You have now."

"And you figure you can handle a four-hitch?"

"I can."

"Well, mebbe. But you ain't gonna handle mine, I can tell you right here and now. I don't hand over the leathers to nobody on my run. How far you going? Tenaha?"

"Right." Gantry figured he could hire or purchase a couple of good mounts there for the last leg of the journey to Jefferson.

"Huh. Right through Foley country, you know."

"Like I said, you can stay here."

"You deaf? I said I'd drive my own run."

"Pride can get you killed."

"Pride? Pride ain't got nary a thing to do with it. I ain't scared of the Foleys. Been held up a half-dozen times this past year. Can't swear it was Foleys done it, but it's a good bet they were in on more than one."

"Have it your way."

"I'm too old and set in my ways to have it any other."

The Thorns were crossing the elm-shaded yard. Joshua was carrying a trunk. Willie followed with the valises. The reinsman helped them load the baggage into the mud wagon's boot. Gantry returned to the porch to fetch Luke Foley. Hannah Malone was standing there.

"He's in no condition to travel, Marshal."

"That's his own doing."

"You don't bend much, do you?"

"Can't afford to. And you can't afford to have him around here too long. We both know that. How much do I owe you for breakfast?"

"Nothing."

"Obliged."

He helped Foley to the mud wagon, then went back to get his saddle. The Thorns had selected the forward bench. The driver heaved the saddle into the luggage boot, strapped down the canvas.

"Carrying a strongbox?" asked Gantry.

"Nope. Just mail bags. But that don't mean we won't get held up. So many road agents in these woods, they have a tough time making a living. Pickings are so slim they might stop you just to steal the shirt off your back."

Gantry noticed the Colt Dragoon stuck in the man's belt.

"Know how to use that horse pistol?"

"Know how to. Also when not to."

Gantry nodded. The driver made it plain where he stood. He wasn't scared of the Foleys, but that didn't mean he was planning to risk his life to help Gantry keep his prisoner, if it came to that.

Gantry put Foley on the rear bench and sat beside him, facing the Thorns. Joshua sat directly across from Luke. He held the revolver in his lap and stared in an unfriendly fashion at Foley. Laura kept her eyes averted, gazing across the neglected fields. She didn't look at all happy. Gantry couldn't blame her. She had seen the dark side of her husband's nature, a side she hadn't realized existed. He thought her rather naive on that score. Everyone had a dark side. Some managed to keep it under control. Some didn't.

As the jehu climbed into the box, Gantry was on the verge of ordering the Thorns to stay behind. He wondered if it wasn't a mistake, permitting them to

39

come along. But before he could make up his mind, the reinsman took up the leathers and whipped the team into motion, and the moment had passed.

Before long the violent up-and-down, side-to-side motion of the mud wagon took its toll on Luke Foley. Ghastly white, drenched in a cold sweat, he suffered terribly. Gantry paid no heed, and Joshua Thorn seemed to derive some satisfaction from Foley's immense discomfort.

"I thought you said you tried to bring them back alive," said Laura, glaring at Gantry.

"I try. Sometimes they don't let me."

"I doubt this man will make it to Tenaha. He's in terrible pain."

"He's got plenty of hard bark. He'll make it."

"But if he doesn't, you won't lose any sleep."

"That's enough, Laura," snapped Thorn.

"What? You want me to behave like a proper lady. Why should I? You haven't exactly been acting like a perfect gentleman of late."

"I never said I was a perfect gentleman."

"There seem to be a number of things you never said to me. It also seems that this is an uncivilized country, and people are expected to act accordingly."

Gantry suppressed a smile. Laura Thorn had spirit. He admired her for it.

"Perhaps," said Thorn stiffly, "you would prefer we return to Virginia."

"Now that you mention it, yes. You know my father would welcome you as a junior partner in his law firm."

"So your father's a lawyer," said Gantry.

"Yes, he is, Marshal. So you will understand when

I tell you that I was brought up believing everyone had certain inalienable rights. Even the prisoners of United States Marshals."

"Yes, ma'am."

"Don't patronize me. I have seen how you treat this man. I've seen dogs treated better."

"He's lucky. There are a lot of lawmen who bring in outlaws belly-down over the saddle. They figure it saves time and trouble, that way." Gantry glanced coldly at Luke. "You talk about rights. I say this one forfeited his rights when he murdered an unarmed horse trader in Jefferson."

"That isn't the way our judicial system works. It isn't your job to decide whether he has forfeited his rights. My husband could tell you as much—except it appears he has forgotten everything he learned."

Foley opened one bleary eye. "You tell 'em, sister," he mumbled weakly. "Give 'em hell."

"So why *do* you try to bring them in alive, Marshal?" badgered Laura. "Why aren't you judge, jury, and executioner, like these other lawmen of whom you speak? I can't believe you actually think he deserves a fair trial before a jury of his peers."

"You're being unfair, Laura," protested Thorn.

"Am I?" Suddenly she relented. "Perhaps. I suppose I should apologize, Marshal. Your job is a difficult and dangerous one. It must make a man cynical and rough."

"It's all I know."

After that, no one spoke for some time. Red dust rose in choking drifts from beneath the iron-rimmed wheels of the mud wagon. They passed through cool green canyons cut into towering pine forests,

41

rumbled across narrow wooden bridges spanning deep ravines hosting sluggish yellow creeks. Patches of swamp were occasionally visible from the trace, gossamer mists clinging to cypress knees.

It was a country completely foreign to Gantry. He missed the wide open spaces. He felt hemmed in, blind, suffocated. In his kind of country the streams danced crystal clear over rocks. The trees were few and far between, each one a work of art, sculpted by a wind that blew strong and clean.

But he'd been ordered here, and he would see the job through.

A telegram had reached him in Fort Worth, where he had been testifying in the trial of the bank robber, Arkansas Tom Ballard. Orders from his superior, Buck Stonecipher, telling him to proceed at once to San Augustine, there to take custody of Luke Foley, wanted on a federal warrant for murder and robbery. On the face of it, a simple task. One Gantry had done many times before. But he had a gut hunch it wasn't going to be quite so simple, this go-round.

Hannah Malone had said twelve miles to Tenaha. Two hours, at this rate. Then two days' ride to Jefferson. Gantry looked forward to the end of the assignment, to the moment he could turn his horse west and make for the high and windswept plains where he belonged.

The road described a long curve, and ahead he saw another deep ravine, another narrow wooden bridge. Joshua Thorn leaned forward suddenly.

"What is it?" asked Gantry.

"Somebody skulking around out there."

Gantry looked, searching the sun-speckled shad-

ows of the forest floor. He saw no one. But he believed Thorn. Joshua's eyes were accustomed to
this terrain.

Leaning out of the wagon, Gantry called on the
driver to pick up the gait. The reinsman lifted a hand
in acknowledgement. Gantry scanned the empty
road ahead.

The bridge exploded.

A ball of orange flame and black smoke, a blast of
searing heat.

The team veered, fighting in their traces, screaming shrilly. One horse went down, felled by shrapnel.
The hitch became a bloody tangled mass of harness
and horse. The stage jolted against the wagon
tongue. The axle splintered, louder than a rifle shot.
The mud wagon careened sideways and tilted crazily,
a violent motion that hurled Gantry clear, an instant
before the stage rolled over.

Chapter Seven

The ground rushed up to meet him. He blacked out, but only for an instant. The crackle of gunfire faded out, then back in. Pushing to his feet, he saw a scatter of still-burning timbers, the remnants of the bridge. Men on horseback were shooting from the trees on both sides of the road. Orange flame spewed from gun barrels.

Gantry started running. A bullet kicked a geyser of dirt in front of him. He veered abruptly to the left. Another bullet scorched the air, too close for comfort. He hurled himself to the ground.

The mud wagon lay on its side directly ahead. Near it was the hitch, what was left of it. One horse was standing. Another lay dead. A third was struggling to stand, but was entangled in the fouled harness, and trying to avoid the flailing hooves of the fourth.

Dust and smoke lay a heavy pall over the scene of the wreck, but not so heavy that Gantry couldn't see the horsemen in the woods. He had no doubt they could see him as well. And they were trying to hit him, with a notable lack of success. It took a damned good shot—or a damned lucky one—to hit a target from horseback, unless the horse happened to be cavalry-trained to stand still in a shooting scrape.

Gantry was gratified to see that these particular horses were not so trained. They pranced and pivoted, and every time a gun went off near their heads, they became even more difficult to handle. The ambushers were forced to concentrate on keeping their mounts under control. As a result, their shooting suffered accordingly.

Their mistake, thought Gantry, for not dismounting. Maybe he could teach them a lesson. He drew his side gun, a single-action Colt .44, sat up, and began methodically returning fire.

He'd been in more gunfights than he could remember. He knew the do's and don't's as well as anyone. He didn't fan the hammer. He didn't shoot just to be shooting. He kept calm, almost detached, and gave no thought to being hit, just to hitting. Each time he fired, he had a target picked. But with their horses acting up, his targets weren't easy. He wounded one of the ambushers in the arm, saw the man slump forward in the saddle.

The horsemen faded back into the trees a bit, but they didn't quit shooting. Gantry counted seven. All were masked, bandannas pulled up to conceal their features.

Laura Thorn cried out. Gantry got up, turned, saw her stumbling away from the wreckage of the mud wagon. In that same instant he saw Luke Foley staggering off in the other direction, making for the trees.

45

"Get down!" yelled Gantry.

The warning was meant for Laura, but she didn't seem to hear him over the gun thunder. She was still reeling around out in the open, and he guessed she was either too stunned by the wreck to think straight, or too panicked by the small-scale war going on all around her. The first time, he knew, was rough on the nerves. It was entirely possible she had never before heard a shot fired in anger.

He made a snap decision. As he ran toward her, he fired in Luke's direction. A rider was coming out of the trees at full gallop, heading for Luke, shooting across the road at Gantry. Everyone was moving fast, and nobody succeeded in hitting anything. The Colt's hammer fell on an empty chamber just as Gantry reached Laura. He hooked an arm around her waist, sweeping her off her feet, and didn't break stride.

The lip of the ravine was straight ahead. He plunged over it, carrying Laura with him, letting go of her as the ground fell away. He landed, rolled, tried to dig his heels in to stop, and hooked a root curling treacherously out of the mud. This pitched him headlong into the creek.

He came up sputtering, searching for the bottom with his feet. The creek was deep. He went under, labored to the surface again. Charred debris from the bridge floated by. He had never been much of a swimmer. Where he came from, the only body of water big enough to swim in had been a stock tank. He managed to dog-paddle gracelessly to the bank, cursed as he realized his Colt lay in the murky depths of the creek.

46

But the fight was over. The shooting had stopped. As he clawed up the muddy bank, he heard the drumbeat of horses on the run, fading quickly.

He cast around for Laura. She too was crawling out of the water. He went to help her, saw a scarlet smear of blood leaking from a bullet graze on her forearm. The sight angered him. The chivalrous bastards hadn't been above shooting at a woman.

He used his bandanna to bind the wound. Her eyelids fluttered. She coughed up a little water, recognized him, clutched feverishly at his arm.

"Joshua . . ." she gasped.

He nodded. "Lay still. I'll find him."

Struggling to the top of the steep embankment, Gantry expected the worst, that Luke Foley had escaped and Joshua Thorn was dead. Foley was gone all right. But to Gantry's surprise, Thorn hadn't answered the final roll call. He came crawling through a tear in the mud wagon's canvas roof. Clear of the overturned stage, he collapsed, unconscious.

Gantry rolled him over, searched for gunshot wounds, and found no evidence. A gash above the left eye was bleeding profusely. A flap of skin, with part of the eyebrow, was hanging loosely.

Laura emerged from the ravine and stumbled forward. She was a sight, drenched from head to toe, her dress torn and covered with red mud. She fell to her knees beside Thorn and looked blankly at the lawman.

"Is he—?"

"He'll be okay. Don't worry."

She bent forward, stretched her arms across Thorn, and rested her head on his chest.

Gantry left them like that and went in search of the driver. The reinsman had been thrown fifty feet. His neck was broken. The Colt Dragoon was still in his belt. Gantry confiscated it.

He checked the horses next. One was dead. Another's leg was fractured. Gantry put this one out of its misery with a single shot. He liberated a third by detaching its tow straps from the singletree. This one he tethered to a wheel of the mud wagon, using the long leather rigging attached to the snaffle bit.

The fourth horse presented a problem. It was thoroughly entangled in harness, down on its side. Gantry searched the pockets of his longcoat, found he hadn't lost the clasp knife that was his only heirloom. The four-inch blade was razor sharp. He liked to keep it that way. His father had. The staghorn grips were carved with the initials J.G.

Cutting the horse loose was no easy task. Gantry had to watch out for flailing hooves. If he got caught in the harness, twelve hundred pounds of wheeler could crush him. The horse lay on its singletree. Rigging had fouled in the tow straps. Gantry sliced the tow straps from the iron hames on the leather collar and pulled them through the loops in the breeching and bellyband. When he cut the rigging, the horse got up and trotted off, apparently none the worse for wear.

Gantry found his rifle. It was still in perfect working order. He was glad of that. The Henry was not the most powerful or most accurate rifle available, but it carried sixteen rounds, more than any other repeater. On a couple of occasions those extra rounds had been the difference between life and death for him.

He went back to the Thorns.

"I'll go for a wagon," he said.

She looked up at him, and he saw that she had been quietly weeping. He felt sorry for her. She'd had one hell of a welcome to Texas.

"I won't be gone long," he promised. "They got what they came for. They won't be back."

"The driver . . ."

He shook his head.

She gazed forlornly at her husband's bloodied face. "He's going to die, isn't he?"

"No. He may be busted up inside. We'll get him to a doctor. But he won't die."

"You don't know that."

"He's strong. I know *that*. And he's got a good reason to live."

"Revenge?"

"No, ma'am. You."

"I said so many harsh words to him. Oh, if I could only take them back."

"What's done is done. You can't change it, so you might as well not worry about it. I'll be back as quick as I can. I hate to leave you, but he can't ride, so we've got to get a wagon. I can't let you go—there's more danger on the road than there is here. Just stay with him. Talk to him."

"He can't hear me."

"He'll hear you." He put the rifle on the ground beside her. "Know how to use this?"

She looked at the Henry as though she didn't know

what it was—like she'd never seen a rifle before.

"Yes," she said. "Yes, of course."

Gantry was dubious, but he said nothing. He went to the horse tied to the wagon. Cutting the long rigging into makeshift reins, he swung aboard Indian fashion. He didn't waste time with his saddle. There was no guarantee the horse would abide a saddle anyway. Time was too precious to waste on experiments. He heeled the animal into a lumbering gallop, heading back along the Trammel Trace for the Malone house. It was the nearest he knew of.

Part of him wanted to be hot on the trail of Luke Foley and the ambushers. He'd never before lost a prisoner, and he had no intention of setting a precedent. But he couldn't leave the Thorns to fend for themselves. He had to see to them first. He'd find help for them. Then he'd get Luke Foley.

Not to mention the bravos who had rescued him. An innocent man lay dead. Every last one of them was going to answer for that.

Gantry decided it was past time the Redlands got a good strong dose of law and order.

Chapter Eight

The first time she'd seen him, coming down the road on foot with his prisoner, Hannah Malone had surmised that Marshal Gantry was double-rectified trouble.

The second time she saw him coming in, exhorting every last whit of speed out of the lathered horse beneath him, she knew it for an ironclad fact. Gantry was trouble, all right, one hundred proof.

As though the Redlands didn't have enough calamity, woe, misfortune, misery, pain, and adversity to go around.

She went out to the road, worried that something had happened to Laura. Gantry explained the situation, speaking curtly, spending words like they were hard-earned dollars. The widow woman was shocked, then outraged. Angry that the stage driver, whom she had known well, had lost his life. No less angry because of the pain, both physical and emotional, that young Laura Thorn was suffering at this very moment.

The boy, Willie, came charging around the house, lured away from his chores by Gantry's arrival. She sent him charging back again, with orders to hitch up the spring wagon.

Gantry had moved past her to the well back up under the tall elms. He cranked the windlass, raising a water-sloshing bucket. As he drank, the bottomed-out horse stepped closer, nudged at the bucket. Gantry let the animal have a taste out of the palm of his hand, wet down the horse's muzzle.

"Did you get a look at them?" asked Hannah.

"They wore masks."

"Luke Foley has three brothers. Matt, Mark, and John. Ma Foley would have planned it. But she can't ride any more. She's a very large woman. Suffers from gout. Just makes her that much meaner. You say they used dynamite to blow up the bridge?"

Gantry nodded, splashing cool water on the back of his neck.

"It was dynamite." He knew the smell. Worse than black powder.

"The Daggetts ride with the Foleys. They're kin. Watt Daggett used to work in the mines as a blaster. Got two boys. Bob and Jesse. Not a dime's worth of difference between them and the Foleys. None worth the pain of the mothers that bore them."

This uncharitable assessment surprised Gantry, coming as it did from Hannah Malone. The widow woman looked abashed.

"Not a very Christian thing to say, was it? Excuse me. I'm just upset."

"Where's the nearest sawbones?"

"Tenaha. Dr. Treadgold. A good man."

"I'll take Thorn on to Tenaha, then. Be obliged for your boy's help. With the bridge gone, I'll have to find another way to get there."

She didn't tell him Willie wasn't her blood. It didn't seem to matter in this instance.

"I'll send him back with the wagon," added Gantry.

The horse was trying to get to the bucket. Gantry pushed the animal away, and dropped the bucket back down into the well. By this Hannah Malone divined that the Marshal expected to do some more hard riding. Too much water and the overheated animal would founder.

"You're going after them?" she asked, though she already knew the answer.

"I am."

"Alone?"

"Thorn said the Tenaha sheriff is a Foley man. Think he'd get up a posse for me?"

"Not likely."

"No, it isn't. So I'll have to do it alone."

He didn't tell her, but he preferred it that way. He didn't have a very high opinion of posses. Made up of amateurs, a posse was usually a liability. It often became a real headache just trying to keep the amateurs alive.

"Against the Foleys and the Daggetts, you won't stand much of a chance," she predicted.

"It's my job."

He was chafing at the bit, suffering every minute of delay. He wanted to be on the trail of Luke Foley and

53

the men who had set Luke free, and he didn't let the odds worry him. The widow woman read this in him, and admired him for it.

"Like as not, Marshal, you'll get lost in the woods," she said, hoping to talk him out of such a risky enterprise, knowing all the while that she was wasting her breath in the attempt. "Men who've lived their entire lives out here sometimes do. If the swamps don't kill you, the Foleys and the Daggetts will. Were anyone to bother looking, they'd never even find your bones."

Gantry shrugged. "Doesn't matter. There's no one to weep over my grave, anyway."

She thought this was the key to the man, the reason for his reckless bravery. He had nothing to hold him back, and nothing to look forward to.

"I can tell you how to find the Daggett place."

That startled him. "Why would you? Beg pardon, ma'am, but I had the idea you didn't want to take sides."

"It isn't healthy, going against the Foleys."

"Then why?"

She looked off across the fields. The mist of sadness drifted across her eyes, obscuring them.

"My husband and oldest son were killed in the war. Ten years ago my youngest was knifed to death in a Tenaha back alley. Robbed. Never found the man or men who did it. Might not have been a Foley or a Daggett. Though that's the kind of thing they would do. Could have been almost anyone. Tenaha has always been that kind of place. A rough dangerous town. But I've wondered, all these years, if it *was* a

54

Foley. Or a Daggett. If it was, and I don't help you now, I've done wrong by my son.''

Gantry wasn't sure he understood the logic, but he could see the resolution in her life-etched features, and could tell it made perfect sense to her.

"Let Willie take the Thorns into Tenaha. You follow that creek east. The one crossed by the bridge that was blown up. It'll run into the Sabine. Turn north. Keep to the river. Four miles or so and you'll see an island. A log jam between the island and the west bank makes a falls. The riverboats use the deep channel east of the island. A half-mile north of the falls, you'll come to another creek, flowing in from the west. Not far up that creek is the Daggett place.

"It's a roundabout way to get there, but the best thing to do in the forest is stick to the creeks and rivers. The Foley place is deeper in the woods, much farther away. Harder to get to. Since Luke is bad hurt, he might hole up at the Daggett's. Besides, they might expect you to come looking for him at the Foley place. Not that they'd expect you, or anyone else, to come looking.''

"Thanks.''

"Don't thank me. I feel like I'm sending you to your death.''

"I'd go anyway.''

"I realize that. Maybe this way you'll accomplish something, other than getting yourself killed. You're a good decent man, Marshal. I admit I wasn't sure of you at first, seeing the way you treated Luke Foley. But you're helping the Thorns, and all the while the men you're after are getting farther away, and that doesn't sit well with you."

Willie drove the spring wagon out to the road, handling the brace of mules with practiced ease. Gantry tied the horse to the tailgate.

"This means war," said Hannah as the lawman climbed onto the seat beside Willie. "Once the Thorns find out what happened to Joshua. Worst thing about war is that the innocent always get hurt. Not just folks who've got no stake in the fight. The widows. The children, too. People like Laura. That's what the people who wage war forget. What they'll have to answer for on Judgment Day. That's another reason I'm helping you, Marshal. I don't know how you'll do it. I doubt you can. But I pray that somehow you'll prevent another war in Shelby County."

He nodded, turned to Willie.

"Let's go. We're burning daylight."

Chapter Nine

Joshua Thorn's condition was neither better nor worse. Laura mournfully informed Gantry that Thorn hadn't regained consciousness during the lawman's absence. Gantry was concerned by this news, but he didn't let on. He reassured her that Thorn would pull through. He sounded much more confident than he felt.

With Willie's help, Gantry got Thorn on the bed of the spring wagon. Willie was strong and rangy, not a boy anymore. He was quiet and plain-featured, the kind of person other people tended to overlook. Gantry watched him closely without seeming to. Willie scanned the scene of carnage with bright-eyed interest. He pocketed spent shell casings, treating them like souvenirs. He helped Gantry cover the body of the reinsman with canvas torn from the roof of the wrecked stage. The corpse didn't seem to bother him at all. He and Gantry put the dead man in the back of the spring wagon, too.

Gantry apologized to Laura for putting her in the

position of having to make the journey in the company of a corpse.

"Wouldn't be right to leave him out here," he explained.

She glanced upward, to the ribbon of blue afternoon sky where buzzards had congregated.

"I understand, Marshal."

"Willie is going to take you to Tenaha, to a doctor there. There's a cutoff back down the road apiece. Willie says it crosses this creek by another bridge and goes on into town. He knows the way."

"And you?"

"I'm going after Luke Foley and the men who did this." He loosened the bandanna dressing on her arm, checked the condition of the bullet graze. "Be sure you get that looked after, ma'am."

"You're going after them alone?"

"Yes, ma'am."

She gazed at him the way people did who knew they were saying good-bye for the last time.

"Now I should apologize, Marshal. For the things I said to you."

He thought, *She doesn't want to make the same mistake twice.*

"You spoke from the heart. Said what you believed. You shouldn't apologize."

"Good luck."

He helped her onto the spring wagon. She sat with Joshua's head in her lap. Her dress was covered with blood and dark mire. In Gantry's opinion, she looked more beautiful than ever. Joshua Thorn was a lucky man. Gantry wondered what it would be like to have someone—especially someone as beautiful as

58

Laura—who cared whether he lived or died.

Telling Willie to wait, he took his saddle from the boot of the overturned stage. Saddlebags were tied to the hull. From these he extracted a box of ammunition for the Henry repeater and a muslin pouch containing jerky and corn dodgers. He loaded the saddle onto the spring wagon.

"If I don't come back," he told Willie curtly, "the saddle's yours."

Willie didn't know what to say, and Gantry didn't give him the time to think of something.

"Get going," he said, and slapped the haunch of the offside mule to motivate the hardtail into motion.

Following Hannah Malone's instructions, Gantry headed east along the creek. The going was anything but easy. Impenetrable tangles of sweetbriar blocked his way. Runoff had gouged deep gullies in the soft red soil of the bank. A thick carpet of pine needles disguised roots and holes, and the horse picked its way carefully.

The sun could scarcely penetrate the thick canopy of towering trees. Wind soughed in the upper reaches, but not a breath of air stirred on the forest floor. It was cold and damp in the eternal woodland shade. Gantry buttoned the mud-caked longcoat and turned up the leather collar.

He rode with the shortened riggings in his right hand and the Henry in his left. The stage driver's Colt Dragoon was in his holster, replacing the pistol he had lost in the creek. He didn't worry about the odds against him, having learned long ago that preoccupations of that kind were not productive. A man who didn't have much of a future, he didn't waste a lot of time wondering what it held in store.

The forest was home to an abundance of wildlife. He caught fleeting glimpses of fox and wild turkey and deer in distant undergrowth. Bluejays and mockingbirds were quick flashes of color in the trees. Gray squirrels berated him as he passed beneath their nests. Snapping turtles and cottonmouths slipped into the murky waters of the creek as he drew near.

Years of manhunting experience had made of him an above-average tracker. More than a few desperadoes had tried without success to throw him off their trail. But he didn't fool himself into believing he could be effective in the Redlands. These trackless forests, spotted with patches of treacherous marsh, were strange to him. The pine needle carpet held no sign. Except at sunrise and sunset, it was almost impossible to keep a sense of direction. There were precious few landmarks. The shadowy woods stretched endlessly in every direction.

The shadows gradually deepened, and by this Gantry realized that the day was drawing to a close. A distant drumroll, thunder, warned him that nightfall would bring rain. Reaching the muddy floodplain of the Sabine River, he saw towering, black-bellied storm clouds filling the darkening sky, quickening the purple twilight.

He followed the west bank of the broad river, finding it easier to walk the horse through the cypress knees. The wind kicked up, chilling him. Then jagged yellow lightning ripped the clouds open, and the cold rain fell in driving sheets, roiling the surface of the Sabine, thrashing the cypress and pine.

Gantry took shelter in the hollowed base of a cypress. He pulled the brim of his hat down low over his face. A torrent of rainwater poured from it. He kept a tight grip on the riggings, keeping the horse close, its head down.

The initial violence of the cloudburst was soon spent. The clouds moved on, and the clearing sky became tinged with the pinks and purples of dusk, seasoned with a sprinkling of early stars.

Gantry pressed on through the dripping forest, keeping the river to his right. His wet clothes chilled him to the bone. Spongy, rank-smelling ground sucked at his boot heels. He longed more than ever for the high desert plains to which he was accustomed.

Long before he saw them, he heard the falls. There, as the widow woman had described, was the wooded island in the middle of the river, and the log jam over which the river crashed. The last of the day's light had been spent. A heavy darkness filled the woodlands. Gantry waited for the early moon. He sat with his back to a cypress, deafened by the tumult of the falls, and ate a strip of jerky and a corn dodger. He drank from the river, and let the horse do likewise. A thousand bullfrogs chorused. A hoot owl questioned the shadows. A crane answered from somewhere on the other side of the river, a ghostly cry.

The moon rose an hour later, laying a sheet of silver upon the surface of the river. Gantry moved on, past the falls, and in short order arrived at the mouth of another creek. This he paralleled, recalling that Hannah Malone had said the Daggett place lay on this run not far from the Sabine. The scent of wood smoke soon verified this, and eventually he saw a speck of light ahead. Lamplight gleaming from a window.

He had to feel his way forward, for the trees were so dense they blocked the moon's fragile light. When close enough to make out the shape of the cabin, he tied the horse to a dogwood. The tree was covered with a profusion of white blooms, so many that the tree was visible from a considerable distance in the indigo blue of the forest night. With the tree as a beacon, he hoped to be able to locate the horse in a hurry if he needed to.

Creeping cautiously forward, Gantry reached a windowless side of the log cabin. He was slipping around the front corner, his destination the lamplit window, when the door creaked open on rusty hinges. Gantry hurried around the corner out of sight. Breathing shallowly, he listened hard. He heard the splash of water, then footsteps in the mud, someone walking away from the cabin. Gantry peeked around the corner in time to see that someone slipping into the gloom-shrouded trees, heading for the creek.

Gantry circled wide around the clearing in front of the cabin, likewise making for the creek. He moved as fast as he dared. Reaching the bank, he stole along it, hearing nothing but the song of the creek.

He almost stepped on the person he stalked, caught a glimpse of shoulder-length yellow hair, a slight frame, a linsey-woolsey shirt belted at the waist with a length of hard-twist. Squatting at the creek's edge, filling a white enamel basin with water, the person heard him and rose, spinning, throwing the basin. Charging through a spray of water, Gantry knocked the basin aside and plowed ahead. The other was already running, quick as greased lightning. Gantry dived, bringing him down, and caught a fist in the eye for his effort.

The Henry repeater was in his hands, but Gantry didn't want to shoot, unless it was absolutely necessary. It would make life a sight easier if he managed to catch the occupants of the cabin by surprise. Apparently this one wasn't armed. This was his chance to cut the odds against him.

Gantry let go of the Henry and got one big hand around his adversary's throat, ready to squeeze off any sound. He used his other hand to block another blow, grabbing a slender wrist and twisting hard, but not hard enough to break bone.

Yellow Hair wasn't very strong or very big. Gantry easily pinned him down, and figured he had a half-grown younker on his hands.

"Be still," he hissed. "Make a sound and I'll snap your neck."

Yellow Hair kept struggling, thrashing like a wildcat in a trap. A knee slammed into Gantry's side. Put out, the lawman squeezed tighter and twisted harder. A choking yelp. The frail body arched beneath him, and Gantry knew he was a short inch away from killing with his bare hands.

Then he realized something else.

Yellow Hair wasn't a man at all, half-grown or otherwise.

Chapter Ten

No doubt about it. He was manhandling a girl.

Just a slip of a girl, really. He didn't have a whole lot of experience with the gentler sex, but he knew a female when he felt one.

Abashed, he got up and pulled her to her feet. She tried to break away. He pinned her against the trunk of a tree.

"Be still," he said, exasperated. "I'm not going to hurt you."

Her eyes glittered like a wild animal's behind a veil of mussed yellow hair. She didn't believe him, and Gantry didn't blame her. After all, a moment before he had been on the verge of breaking her arm and choking the life out of her.

He took a closer look. She wore the man's shirt like a dress. Her legs and feet were bare. Her face and arms and legs were smudged with dirt, her feet caked with mud. She'd been a long time unwashed and underfed. It was difficult to tell in the dark, with any certainty, how old she was.

"Who are you?" he asked.

"Mercy."

"That's your name?"

She nodded.

"Mercy what?"

"Just Mercy."

"Are you a Daggett?"

She shook her head.

"Isn't this the Daggett place?"

She nodded again.

"So what are you doing here?"

She thought it over. "I live here."

She wasn't a Daggett, but she lived here. Gantry was curious, but there were more pressing matters to attend to, and getting information out of her was about as easy as pulling teeth.

"Who's in the cabin?"

"Watt Daggett. His boys, Bob and Jesse. Bob's hurt."

"How hurt?"

"Gunshot."

"Luke Foley. Is he in there?"

Again she shook her head. "The Foleys are gone. They were here today, but they're gone now."

"*Mercy!*"

The shout came from the cabin. Looking through the trees, Gantry saw a man standing in the doorway, silhouetted against the light inside. Gantry doubted the man could see them, at this distance and in the creek-side thicket.

"Mercy! Get your butt back here with that water!"

"That's Watt Daggett," she whispered. "He sent me down here to fetch more water. He's dug the bullet out of Bob's arm. I got to go, or he'll figure something's not right."

Gantry realized he was in a bad spot. If he didn't let her return to the cabin, the Daggetts would be alerted. If he did, she would probably warn them.

"Mercy! Dammit, you best—"

"I'm coming!" she yelled.

Watt Daggett turned back inside.

"I won't tell 'em, mister," she said. "I swear I won't."

"Why not?"

"You after the Daggetts?"

"Yes. The Foleys, too."

"You the one put the bullet in Bob Daggett?"

"Yes."

"I wish you'd shot straighter."

Gantry considered the implications of that remark. She sounded sincere. But he still wasn't sure he could trust her. Possibly she was putting on an act in order to get loose and warn the Daggetts. Why would she side with him, and not the Daggetts?

He wasn't convinced, but he was out of time. He had to make a decision.

He let go of her, expecting her to bolt, screaming at the top of her lungs.

Instead, she stood there, watching him, brushing hair out of those big, glittering eyes. Intense, unblinking eyes.

"Okay," he said. "Go on."

"Are you the law, mister?"

He pulled his longcoat aside. A sliver of moonlight glanced off the ball-pointed badge pinned to his shirt.

"I won't tell 'em," she promised.

"Sure."

"I won't. What are you going to do?"

"You'll find out."

"You alone?"

"No."

"You're alone," she said, nodding.

He had never been able to lie very convincingly.

"If there's shooting," he said, "stay the hell down and out of the way."

She retrieved the basin and filled it with water. As she passed him, heading back to the cabin, she gave him a long look. Gantry thought he saw the ghost of a smile playing at the corners of her small mouth, but he couldn't be certain in the darkness.

Watching her go, he considered his options. There weren't many, and none were too appealing. Despite her earnest assurances, it was a good bet she would raise the alarm once she reached the cabin. But what could he do about her? Either let her go or silence her. And to harm a woman cut against his grain. That he had done so inadvertently troubled him.

The odds against him were three to one. Maybe more. He had only Mercy's word for it that the cabin held just Watt Daggett and his two sons. Without the element of surprise, it wouldn't be easy dealing with three desperate characters.

He thought about retreat, discarded the notion. Never had he backed down. A lawman couldn't afford to, not even once. If he did, just one time, to save his skin, he was good as dead. Maybe still walking around breathing air, but a dead man nonetheless. A lawman's reputation was his greatest asset. Many a hardcase would back down from a badge-toter he knew would keep on coming on, no matter what.

And there was a personal factor, too. A man who surrendered to fear on one occasion, would find it easier to rationalize the same course of action the next time his life was threatened. Cowardice was habit-forming.

So he couldn't beat a hasty retreat. And he couldn't wait out here for them. He didn't relish the thought of tackling three outlaws who knew these woods much better than he, prowling through the night with blood in their eyes.

Picking up the Henry, Gantry pushed through the thicket, emerged into the clearing, and with long strides made for the cabin doorway.

He was three steps from it when a man suddenly appeared there. Gantry looked for weapons, saw none. The man's eyes widened. He opened his mouth to yell. Gantry closed swiftly, hammering the stock of the rifle into the man's gut. The man doubled over, wheezing. Gantry laid the Henry's barrel across his skull. The man slammed into the door frame, reeled inside, and collapsed.

Gantry stepped over him and into the cabin, his finger on the trigger.

Chapter Eleven

The cabin was one room. The furniture consisted of a split-log table, a couple of chairs over by the stone fireplace, three narrow rope-slat bunks along the walls. A woodburner stood in one corner. Several rifles and shotguns leaned in another. A couple of crates were nailed to the walls, containing canned goods. Bear skins covered a puncheon floor. Wolf pelts and deer antlers decorated the walls. Wooden shutters in windows front and back were open, despite the damp chill of the night.

Gantry had trained himself to see everything in a glance when he stepped into a room. It wasn't enough to focus on the occupants. You had to know where the doors and windows were located, and the furnishings. All these factors could become important if the situation took a bad turn.

A young man sat at the table, shirtless. Blood streaked his arm, pooling on the floor. He was bent forward, his head resting on the table, the injured arm dangling. Gantry's violent entrance brought him bolt upright. He grabbed for a pistol lying on the table.

An older man stood near the fireplace. Mercy was near him, bending down to feed a fire which crackled hotly. Flames licked at the blackened bottom of an iron kettle dangling from a hearth hook. The older man whirled to face Gantry. The lawman caught a glimpse of the knife a split second before the man 'hurled the weapon.

With one man throwing a Bowie and the other reaching for his shooting iron, Gantry didn't have time to think. Reflex took over. Before the knife left the older man's hand, the marshal was falling into a quick roll which brought him close to the end of the table. As he rose, he overturned the table. The wounded man was knocked backward, pitching to the floor. He cried out in pain and lost his grip on the pistol, which skittered away.

The older man—Gantry assumed this to be Watt Daggett—spun toward the stack of long guns in the near corner. Mercy swung an iron poker and knocked his feet out from under him. He landed flat on his face. Gantry took two long strides, sweeping the Henry's stock to shoulder. Watt reached for the rifles and shotguns.

"Do it and I'll kill you," said Gantry.

He spoke softly. Sudden death put a razor's edge to every syllable. Watt Daggett, being the old hand and born survivor that he was, froze.

"Look out!" yelled Mercy.

Gantry spun. Watt and the wounded man were in front of him, so the only source of danger left was the Daggett he had plowed over coming through the doorway. The door was closed now; the man was on his feet, reaching for gun rigs hanging on wooden pegs driven into the wall behind the door. Gantry hadn't seen these. The open door had previously hidden them from view.

"Don't try it," warned Gantry.

The man didn't seem to hear. A pistol came clear of holster leather. The man turned, bringing the gun to bear. Gantry fired. The repeater spat flame. The rimfire bullet struck dead center, the impact lifting the man off his feet, hurling him backwards. He was dead before he hit the floor.

Hearing Watt Daggett's snarl of rage, Gantry turned back to confront the old man. He was certain he had nothing more to fear from the man he had just shot. He didn't need to check a pulse to know the man was dead. Many men were faster than Gantry, but none were as deadly accurate.

Watt was going for the guns again. Gantry could have stopped him permanently, but he lived by one hard, fast rule. He never shot to kill unless the other man had a weapon in hand. Watt Daggett was a heartbeat away from qualifying. Gantry didn't let him. The butt of the Henry came down hard on Watt's skull. Watt collapsed, out like a candle in a hurricane.

"Pa!" The wounded Daggett, Bob, crawled weakly across the floor, trying to reach his father, leaving a smear of scarlet on the worn wood.

Gantry stepped over him, took up the pistol Bob had dropped, laid it on the table. He removed the rifles and shotguns from the corner, placed them on the table as well. The guns and rigs on the wall pegs

behind the door were added to this collection, as wa
the Bowie knife, embedded in the wall. An old
fowling piece hung above the fireplace. Gantry took
it down. He looked at Mercy.

"Any more?"

She removed two pistols from beneath a thin
mattress, contributed them to the pile of hardware.

"Enough artillery here to start a war," remarked
Gantry.

"There is a war," replied Mercy. "A feud."

"So I've heard. What's in those crates under the
bunk yonder?"

She slid one of the crates out, extracted a stick of
dynamite, held it up for him to see.

"Be careful with that," he breathed.

She smiled. "Don't worry. It isn't very dangerous
without a blasting cap."

Gantry realized this was so. He was no expert, but
he knew that the explosive element in dynamite was
nitroglycerin, by itself highly volatile. Mixed with
chalk and other inert substances, nitro could be
stabilized. Dynamite sticks could be cut and molded
without risk. Copper blasting caps containing
fulminate of mercury were commonly used to ignite
them.

"Watt keeps it bedded down in straw and strips of
burlap," explained Mercy. "In case it starts to sweat.
That's when it can hurt you."

"You know about dynamite, do you?"

She looked across the cabin at Watt Daggett. On her
face was an odd expression Gantry couldn't fathom.

"I been around long enough to learn, just hearing
them talk, and watching them. A little while ago,

Watt was hollering at Jesse for cutting the fuses too long today. Said Jesse nearly blew Luke Foley to kingdom come."

"Not to mention a few others."

"That when you shot Bob?"

"Yes."

"Now you've killed Jesse." She glanced at the dead man, back to Watt, finally up at Gantry. "You better shoot Watt Daggett right now, mister."

"Can't do that."

"Won't nothing short of a bullet in the brainpan keep Watt from killing you, after what you done."

"I'll cross that bridge when I come to it."

She put the stick of dynamite back in the box, rose, and went to the table, where she selected a pistol.

"What are you doing?" asked Gantry.

"If you don't shoot him, reckon I'll have to."

He wrenched the gun out of her grasp.

"You're a strange one," he said brusquely. "You're not afraid of dynamite. Or murder."

She stared at him, impassive. Now, in the lamplight, he could see that her eyes were a deep violet, the color of the western sky at twilight. Her face was oval, with a sharp chin and prominent cheekbones. The nose was pert and slightly up-turned. Her mouth was small and round, with a hairline scar at the corner. Those large, arresting eyes, in a small face with such small features, gave her an elfin appearance.

The way she stared disconcerted him. Gantry liked to think he could read most people. But he had no idea what was going through her mind at this moment. She was an odd one. Still, there could be no denying she had helped him. Maybe even saved his bacon.

"Look," he said, gentling his tone. "They're in my custody. I want them alive. Okay?"

"Okay. But Watt's gonna try to kill you. Me, too."

"Let me worry about Watt Daggett."

"Then you'd best tie him up 'fore he comes to. Watt has a hard head."

"I'll do that. You unload all these guns and toss the ammunition out the door."

She did as he asked. Gantry found some rope. He bound Watt's hands behind his back. He tied Bob Daggett up as well. Bob was sitting next to his father, and glowered, tight-lipped.

"I'll dress that arm for you," said Gantry.

Bob spat in his face.

Gantry's fist connected with the point of Bob's chin. The younger Daggett's eyes rolled in their sockets. He hit the back of his head a good lick on the floor, but he didn't feel it. He was already out cold.

Gantry sleeved spittle off his chest. Mercy came over to kneel beside Watt and check the bindings.

"Good enough?" asked Gantry, amused.

"I guess."

"Any whiskey around here?"

"You're not a drunkard, are you?"

"What kind of question is that? Whiskey's good as anything for cleaning wounds."

"Watt says likker and dynamite don't mix."

"He's got a point. Well, then. I'll need a blade heated in the fire, and hot water. Something clean to use for a dressing."

She nodded, stood. Gantry inspected Bob Daggett's wound. The bullet had been cut out. Watt had probably been heating the blade of the Bowie knife to use in the cauterization. Gantry's untimely arrival had cost Bob a lot of blood.

Mercy hadn't moved, gazing earnestly at him.

"What is it?" he asked.

"You gotta take me with you, mister."

"You'd be better off staying here."

"No, I wouldn't."

Gantry sat back on his heels, puzzled.

"You say you're not a Daggett, but you've been living with them for a spell. How is that? You kin to them?"

Mercy shook her head. "Ain't got no kin. Well, I got a pa. Somewhere. I don't rightly know where. He lit out a couple years back, after my ma died of the fever. Pa . . . drank too much. Folks said he wasn't good for much of nothing. He didn't want to take me with him when he took off. Said he didn't want to have to look out for me. That I'd just slow him down. So he . . . he sold me to Watt Daggett for the price of a case of whiskey."

Gantry looked away from those intense violet eyes. He felt sorry for her. Angry, too. A father who would sell his daughter for whiskey money was scarcely fit to live. And Gantry felt none too charitable when it came to Watt Daggett. He didn't need it spelled out to know for what purpose Watt had purchased Mercy.

"All right," he said. "I'm taking these two into Tenaha. You can come with me that far. After that, you'll be on your own."

Because after that, he thought, *I'll be going after the Foleys.*

75

Chapter Twelve

Gantry cleaned and dressed Bob Daggett's wound. Watt regained consciousness. The lawman made father and son sit in a corner far from the door.

"I don't care to lie on the floor like a damned cur dog," growled Watt.

He was a big man, thick through the chest and shoulders. His eyes were dark, almost black, recessed deeply beneath bushy jutting brows. Reflecting the flames in the fireplace, they looked like burning embers in the black pit of Hell. His hair was the color of rusted iron. His beard was as dense and tangled as a sweetbriar thicket. Gantry couldn't see his lips move when he spoke.

"You make me sleep on the floor," said Mercy.

Those hellfire eyes fastened on her.

"I know what you done. I won't forget."

Mercy glanced anxiously at Gantry. He could tell she was afraid of Watt Daggett. Deathly afraid. He figured she had good reason to be. Watt appeared to be a harsh, brutal, volatile man. An unfeeling man, too. One of his sons lay dead, and Watt displayed less emotion than a stone statue.

"Don't worry," Gantry told her. "He can't hurt you now. I won't let him."

"You won't let me?"

Gantry heard a sound like the rustle of dry leaves. Watt was chuckling.

"Better get your things together, Mercy," said Gantry. "We'll be going at first light."

"I ain't got any things."

He glanced at her bare legs and feet. "What about clothes? Don't you have any?"

She shook her head.

"Then try to get some rest."

She looked around the cabin. At the body of Jesse Daggett, the blood on the floor, the guns on the table, Watt still glaring at her.

"Use one of the bunks," suggested Gantry.

"Where you taking us at first light, lawman?" asked Watt.

"You're under arrest, Daggett. You and your son. I'm taking you to Tenaha."

"Tenaha? That'll work. That'll work just fine."

"If you think the sheriff there will be able to help you, think again."

Watt didn't respond. He proceeded to glower at Mercy again. She lay, curled up tightly, on one of the bunks.

"Stop that," said Gantry.

Watt kept staring, as though he thought he might be able to kill her with his eyes.

Mercy had torn some cloth into strips to use as bandages. A few strips were left over. Gantry selected two, went to the Daggetts, and blindfolded Bob.

"What do you think you're doing?" rasped Watt.

Gantry blindfolded him.

He sat at the table, watching the Daggetts, listening to the chorus of bullfrogs and crickets in the night, the crackle of the fire in the hearth. The flames gradually died down. A chill invaded the cabin. Gantry closed the window shutters. He took a blanket from one of the unoccupied bunks and covered Mercy. She was still awake, trembling. Not from the cold. She was watching Watt Daggett, wide-eyed. Gantry could understand her wanting to kill him. You killed a rattlesnake without second thought, whether it presented an immediate danger or not.

He laid a comforting hand on her shoulder.

"You're safe, Mercy."

"I ain't. I ain't safe long as he's breathing."

"Why didn't you run away?"

"You don't think I tried? He run me down. Beat me so bad I couldn't move for days. After a while I quit tryin', or he would have beat me to death."

"Ain't nothing compared to what I'm *gonna* do," said Watt, across the cabin.

Gantry started for him, but Mercy grabbed his wrist.

"No. Please. Stay close to me, mister."

His heart went out to her. He sat on the edge of the bunk. She wouldn't let go of his wrist. He didn't try to pull away. In time she fell asleep.

Though bone-tired, Gantry stayed awake and alert, watching the Daggetts by the light of the kerosene lamp on the table. Bob Daggett regained consciousness, stirred restlessly for a while, then surrendered to sleep. Watt Daggett never moved. Gantry could almost see those hellfire eyes through the blindfold.

The night crept slowly by. Gantry was accustomed to long vigils. He figured he could catch up on lost sleep in the grave.

The gray dawn slipped through holes in the cabin walls. Gantry tried to extricate himself from Mercy's grasp without waking her, and failed. She sat bolt upright. How many mornings, he wondered, had she awakened in the grip of fear? The years of terror spent here had left deep scars.

"Horses?" he asked.

"In a lean-to, out back."

"How many?"

"Three."

He asked her to saddle them and bring them around to the front of the cabin. She nodded and ran to do his bidding. He didn't blame her for being in a hurry to leave.

He removed the blindfolds from the Daggetts, got them to their feet, and marched them outside. As he passed the body of Jesse Daggett, he grabbed an arm and dragged the corpse out after him. He ordered Watt and Bob to sit on the ground, scanned the surrounding woods. He saw no evidence of planting or plowing. The Daggetts made a living from less honest work.

"Any particular place you want your son buried, Daggett?" he asked.

"In the ground."

Gantry found a shovel leaning against the cabin

wall, alongside an axe and a few traps. He dug a shallow grave ten paces from the cabin. As he worked, Mercy arrived with three saddled horses. Good-looking stock. He wondered where the Daggetts had stolen them. Sending Mercy after his own horse, he finished the grave and put the mortal remains of Jesse Daggett into it.

"Want to say words over him?" he asked Watt, when he'd finished covering the body and tamping down the dirt.

Watt nodded curtly.

Gantry got him to his feet and escorted him to the edge of the grave. Watt regarded it, from one end to the other, flattened a couple of dirt clods with his boot heel.

"Ashes to ashes. Dust to dust," he murmured, dispassionately. "Reckon you're gone to Hell, Jesse. Never was much doubt on that score. Leastways, I know we'll meet again. You weren't good for much of nothing except putting away the vittles, but you were my own flesh and blood and I . . ." Watt shook his head fiercely. "You were about as dim-witted as a possum, and that's the nicest thing I can think to say about you. You weren't long for this world, but maybe you'll feel better about the sorry way it ended by knowin' that the man who killed you ain't long for it, either."

Watt looked across the grave at Gantry.

The lawman's smile was sardonic.

"Well, that was a damned fine eulogy," said Gantry. "Now let's ride."

Chapter Thirteen

It took the entire day to reach Tenaha. Gantry found his way out of the forest by retracing his steps, following in reverse the route Hannah Malone had imparted to him. Reaching the Trammel Trace, he decided to stick to the woods and travel parallel to the road rather than on it. He used their own bandannas to gag Watt and Bob Daggett, not wanting them to call out if any of their friends or fellow road agents passed on the trace.

A man in a wagon, a lone horseman, and then a pair of riders appeared on the road that day. Each time, Gantry stopped and put his horse alongside Watt's—and the Colt Dragoon alongside Watt's head. They remained undiscovered by the passersby.

Gantry felt these precautions were justified; he wasn't going to lose any more prisoners. Better safe than sorry. It was possible that any stranger met would turn out to be kin or cohort of the Daggetts. And it was a lead-pipe cinch that he, Gantry, couldn't expect to meet any friends in these parts.

The Daggetts rode all day with hands tied behind their backs. The long ride took its toll on the wounded Bob. He fell once, getting snagged in a briar thicket and pulled out of the saddle. Gantry got him back aboard and hooked his belt over the saddlehorn.

Later in the day Watt Daggett started falling off his horse. After the second tumble, Gantry began to suspect the wily old renegade of subterfuge. Watt was doing his best to slow them down. Gantry wondered if he had reason to think there might be pursuit.

He asked Mercy about it. "Any chance somebody would go by the Daggett cabin today?"

"Maybe. Men come by all the time."

"Who?"

"If they were good, God-fearing folk, they wouldn't come calling on the Daggetts," she replied. "These woods are chock full of wanted men, mister. Some just show up to shoot the breeze. Sometimes they come to buy dynamite from Watt."

Gantry nodded. If a wild bunch used dynamite in a bank holdup or railroad job in Shelby County, they probably got the stuff from Daggett.

"How did he come by all that dynamite, anyway?" he asked.

Mercy shrugged. "He used to work in a mine. Stole it, I guess."

"That wouldn't surprise me."

His immediate concern was the fact that if someone did show at the Daggett place, the word would go out in a hurry that the Daggetts had been taken away by force. The blood and the fresh grave would vouch for that. Gantry began to pay more attention to their back trail. And when Watt fell for the third time and pretended to be hurt, Gantry issued a stern warning.

"You keep this up and I'll tie you belly-down across the saddle, friend. Men have been known to die if made to ride too long like that. It's your call."

Watt had no reason to doubt Gantry would carry out the threat. He fell no more that day.

They arrived at Tenaha without mishap.

The crimson and gold colors of sunset could not disguise the drab and dreary aspect of the town. Tenaha was nestled in a hollow surrounded by pine-covered hills. A creek skirted the south edge of town. The main street was rutted and wide—wide enough to permit the turnaround of a wagon and team. The narrow cross streets were little better than alleys, overgrown with weeds and sour with trash. The buildings were made of logs or raw board.

Lamplight poured out of windows and doors, throwing yellow rectangles across the main street. Of the twenty-odd structures facing the street, six housed saloons. These watering holes were the focus of the evening's activities. The tinny cascade of a piano issued from one, the screeching caterwaul of a fiddle from another. The sounds of men drunk or in the process rumbled across the street. Dark shapes clotted the boardwalks.

Gantry's arrival with Mercy and the Daggetts did not go unnoticed. The lawman was in the lead, Watt and Bob riding side by side behind him. Gantry had hold of their reins. Mercy brought up the rear. But as the men began to gather on the rim of the street, Gantry called her to him.

"We better part company now," he told her. "Looks like trouble brewing."

"But what will I do? Where will I go?"

He sympathized with her. But he had a job to do, and the job would be that much tougher if he had to look out for her.

"I don't know," he said, more gruffly than he intended. "Stay clear of me, though. You'll get hurt if you don't."

She checked her horse and let him go on. He didn't look back. Though he didn't know why he should be, he felt ashamed.

On both sides of the street men began to move parallel with them, keeping on or close to the boardwalks. A grim undercurrent of whispered talk reached Gantry. One soul, braver or perhaps more belligerent than the rest, broke from the crowd and quartered across the street toward the riders. He was a tall, bearded character, wearing a red flannel shirt, cord trousers, and mule-ear boots. He carried a knife and a pistol in his wide leather belt, and was a fair representative of the others. Tenaha was a favorite rendezvous of freighters, rivermen, and lumberjacks.

The man squinted through the deepening dark at the Daggetts.

"That you, Watt?"

Watt's mumbled response was incomprehensible; he and his son were still gagged.

The man fell in step alongside Watt's horse.

"Stand away," said Gantry.

"What's going on?"

Gantry turned his horse, used it as a wedge between the man and Watt Daggett.

"Looking for trouble tonight?" asked Gantry, pleasantly.

The man stood his ground. He and his kind weren't ones to scare easy.

"What are you?" he asked, surly. "Bounty hunter?"

"United States Marshal."

"That so?" said the man, sarcastically. "Didn't recollect we was in the United States."

"I'm here as a reminder."

The man snorted and angled back to the mob on the boardwalk. Gantry proceeded up the street, the Daggetts in tow.

The jail appeared on his right, a log cabin with strap-iron on the windows. A storm lantern, hanging from a nail beside the door, threw its amber light on wanted posters tacked to the front wall with horseshoe nails. Gantry noticed that one poster was not official issue. A newspaper photograph of Ulysses S. Grant had been glued to a piece of paper. Above the photograph was the word REWARD. Below it was the inscription WANTED DEAD OR ALIVE—10,000 CONFEDERATE DOLLARS.

Grant was no longer President, but during his two terms in office, the Occupation had brought a great deal of hardship and injustice down upon Texas. Gantry figured that had something to do with this homemade wanted poster.

For the first time, he began to realize the full dimensions of what he was up against. These people weren't going to be quick about recognizing any authority other than their own. And apparently, even after all these years, Rebel sentiment still ran high in the Redlands. He represented not only law and order, but also the United States of America—two strong marks against him.

Checking his horse in front of the jail, he dismounted, tied the horse to the hitch rail, and got the Daggetts off their mounts. The mob was gathering, crowding the boardwalk, forming a dense circle of antagonism in the street.

Worse, Mercy was still with him. She sat her horse, looking at him with a quiet desperate resolve.

"Get down," he snapped, suppressing a bitter anger.

He turned his back on her, not waiting to see if she obeyed. Her presence was a dangerous distraction.

Jabbing Watt in the lower spine with the Henry's barrel, he pushed the older Daggett toward the jail. Bob, weakened by the long ride and his gunshot wound, staggered. Hostile murmurs rippled through the crowd. Watt, sensing that the situation was rapidly turning in his favor, stopped dead in his tracks and glanced over his shoulder at Gantry, eyes ablaze with defiance. At the same time, several men moved to block the door of the jail.

Gantry pushed relentlessly forward, hammering the Henry into Watt's back, between the shoulder blades, a blow that propelled Daggett headlong into the men blocking the way. Snatching Bob by the shirt collar, Gantry plowed on through. A man fell, another cursed. Gantry reached the door, praying it wasn't locked. It wasn't. The door swung inward. He tossed Bob inside, turned to grab Watt and drag him in as well. Both Daggetts ended up in a pile on the floor. Gantry commanded the doorway, rifle leveled at the hip.

"Make way for the lady, boys," he said.

They separated, letting Mercy through. Gantry took a quick scan of the jail's interior. A front room with a kneehole desk, stove, and gunrack, two cells of strap iron in the back. No prisoners in the cells, no sheriff in the office.

A man was trying to come through the door. Gantry stiff-armed him back out onto the boardwalk.

"Who the hell do you think you are?" asked a surly member of the mob.

"Said it before. U.S. Marshal."

"We don't want your kind around here."

"Yeah, we take care of our own problems," seconded another.

Shouts of accord rose up, sharp with rancor. The crowd was getting rowdy. Gantry had gotten the best of them so far, and that rankled. So did his glacial calm. But Gantry had faced angry mobs before. They didn't intimidate him. As long as he displayed resolve, he held the upper hand. A mob was like a wolf pack. You had a good chance unless you showed weakness. Show fear, if only for an instant, and you were done for. Falter, hesitate, and they were on you, tearing you to pieces.

He figured most of these men weren't so much *for* the Daggetts, as they were *against* him. He was an outsider. Worse than that, a badge-toter. They were gathered to take his measure—freeing the Daggetts would just be icing on the cake. He had to show them there was no profit in taking him on.

So he stepped boldly out among them again, looking the closest men square in the eye, one after another. Reaching over, he tore the homemade wanted poster featuring Ulysses S. Grant off the wall.

The mob fell silent. Gantry's gall surprised them, threw them off balance. They couldn't help but be impressed by such cool audacity in the face of odds so steep.

"This man was President of these United States," said Gantry. "Like it or not, *your* president. Let's show a little respect."

A man hawked and spat. He was careful to turn his head when he did, and the spittle landed nowhere near Gantry.

"That's what ten thousand dollars Confederate is worth these days," remarked Gantry.

"Damned Yankee," mumbled someone in the rear of the crowd.

"I'm a Texan," said Gantry, turning back inside the jail. "And if this street isn't cleared in ten minutes, I'll have to come back out here and prove it."

Chapter Fourteen

Before the ten minutes was up, the Tenaha sheriff arrived. Gantry had been expecting him. Linus Hoag was a short paunchy individual. The only imposing thing about him was his belly. His legs were stumpy, his feet absurdly small, his shoulders virtually nonexistent. He seemed to have a tough time keeping his gun belt from sliding off his rotund midsection and down to his knees. His cheeks were mottled, his nose crosshatched with broken veins, his eyes bloodshot. He reeked of snakehead whiskey.

"You the sheriff?" asked Gantry, sitting behind the desk.

He'd asked the same question five minutes earlier of another man stepping through the door. That man had glowered belligerently, hitching at his gunrig. He had answered no, defiantly, and given a furtive glance at the Daggetts in one of the strap-iron cells. Gantry had fired the Colt Dragoon without giving the man time to state his business. The half-ounce slug had drilled the door frame, and the man had lost his nerve and beat a hasty retreat.

"Can't you see this here tin star?" asked Hoag, thumbing the badge on his shirt.

"A badge doesn't make a sheriff," replied Gantry.

"Well, I'm the sheriff all right. This is my jail, and that's my desk, dammit," snapped Hoag, truculently.

Gantry didn't budge, apparently in no hurry to return either the desk or the building to the custody of its rightful owner. He turned his attention instead to the man who had accompanied Linus Hoag—a tall, cadaverous gentleman with a severe countenance, clad in somber black attire.

"Who are you?"

"Ezekiel Cravens, suh," replied the man, his deep voice imbued with a stern and disapproving tone. "I am the duly elected judge of Shelby County, as Mr. Hoag is the duly elected sheriff of Tenaha."

"So we'd like to know who the hell you think you are," said Hoag, "coming in here like this and taking over my jail."

Gantry held open his longcoat to give them a glimpse of his badge.

"Gantry, United States Marshal. I wasn't duly elected by a living soul. The State of Texas saw fit to give me this appointment. In other words, I earned this job, I didn't pay for it."

Cravens waxed indignant. "I don't believe I care for what you are implying, suh."

"We'll worry about that later," said Gantry. "Right now I think you ought to send someone for a doctor."

Cravens glanced at the cell. It was evident that Bob

Daggett was feeling more than a little peaked, after such a long ride in a gunshot condition. The younger Daggett sat slumped forward on one of the narrow bunks in the cell. Watt stood at the cell door, watching the goings-on with blazing eyes. Father and son were still gagged and bound.

"Is he badly hurt?" asked Cravens, concerned.

"He'll live. It isn't for him we'll be needing the doctor."

"Who then?"

Gantry stood, Colt Dragoon in hand.

"I gave that mob out there ten minutes to disperse. Reckon time's up."

As he started around the desk, Cravens held up a hand.

"No need for violence, suh. They will heed my counsel."

"Be my guest."

Cravens stepped outside to deal with the hostile crowd. Gantry was more than willing to give the judge his chance at peacemaking. With no sleep the night before, and precious little the night before that, Gantry was bone-tired. He had grit behind his eyes and a short fuse on the powder keg of his Irish temper. He was not in a very civilized mood.

Hoag crossed to the cell.

"Don't worry none, Watt, we'll get this squared away." He turned on Gantry. "How come you got 'em trussed like turkey come Thanksgiving?"

"I had a hunch Watt Daggett wasn't going to come along peaceably, were I to ask him polite-like."

"Watt here is a fine man. Known him for many a year. There must be some mistake."

"I admire the way you stand up for your constituents, Sheriff."

Judge Cravens came back inside.

"Those men have gone about their business. I ask you not to judge them too harshly, suh. The Daggetts have many friends."

"I noticed."

"What are you doing here?" Hoag directed this curt query at Mercy, who stood with her back to the wall, behind the desk, trying to remain inconspicuous. The sheriff seemed to recognize her. Watt made angry noises. Mercy glanced fearfully from behind the veil of yellow hair at Gantry.

"She's with me," said Gantry, crossly. "Leave her alone."

"I must insist you remove the gags from your prisoners," Cravens said.

"Go ahead. You can feed 'em, read to 'em, pray for 'em, and tuck 'em in, for all I care. But the one thing you better not do is cut 'em loose."

"I am acquainted with the law," replied Cravens stiffly. "I realize they are federal prisoners. But the sheriff and I have the right to know why two of our most respected citizens are being treated in this manner."

"They aided in the escape of another federal prisoner."

"Who?" asked Hoag.

"Like you didn't know. Luke Foley. In the process, an innocent man lost his life. A stage driver."

"You saw these two men at the scene of the crime?" asked Cravens.

"There were seven or eight riders. All wore masks.

But I know Watt and his boy were there. I tracked them down."

"But you cannot say with absolute certainty that one of them was directly responsible for the driver's death."

"Don't play games, Judge," admonished Gantry. "Every one of those riders can be charged with murder, and I intend to see it done."

Cravens glanced again at the cell. "Where is Jesse?"

"I killed him," said Gantry.

"It was self-defense," Mercy hastened to add.

Cravens's brittle glare pinned her to the wall. "Is this woman going to serve as your witness, Marshal?"

"That's up to her."

Gantry realized what a dangerous situation this was for her, and he wasn't going to force her to help him. Cravens, Hoag, the mob whose ugly presence had filled the dark street moments ago—all these men were Daggett allies. If she turned against Watt, they would become her mortal enemies. Gantry wasn't worried about the odds for himself; he'd high-stepped over stiff odds before. But what chance would a defenseless wisp of a girl have against a town full of rough and violent men?

"Well," said Cravens, "that strikes me as being of no consequence at this stage. What are your intentions, suh?"

"I want these two held here. I'm going after Luke Foley tomorrow. I'll expect the Daggetts to be right where I leave them when I get back."

"You going after Luke Foley, alone?" asked Hoag,

wearing a crooked grin. "What if you don't get back? You take on one Foley, you take 'em all on. No man has done that and lived to tell the tale."

"If I thought it wouldn't be a waste of time, I'd try to get a posse together."

"You won't find too many men who'll ride against the Foleys," said Hoag, gloating.

Gantry had broached the subject just to test the water. Hoag was only confirming what Hannah Malone had already said.

"Oh, well," said Gantry, sardonic. "You want a job done right, you do it yourself."

"Do you have a federal warrant to arrest these men?" asked Hoag, thumbing over his shoulder at the Daggetts.

Gantry smiled at Cravens. "Is he kidding?"

"Actually, he has a valid point," replied the judge. "You did not apprehend them at the scene. You pursued them without a warrant."

"We know how to get technical when it suits us, don't we? Okay, let's say I had a warrant. Six of them. Right here." Gantry brandished the Colt Dragoon. "Six .44 caliber warrants. Will that do?"

"You're a disgrace to the badge you wear, Gantry," sneered Hoag.

"You're an expert on the subject of disgrace, are you, Hoag?"

"Gentlemen, gentlemen." Judge Cravens held up his hands, his tone positively dulcet. "We are all on the same side here."

"What side might that be?" asked Gantry, hot under the collar.

"Why, the side of law and order, suh. Naturally."

"Sounds to me, Judge," said Hoag, "like this feller is the kind who takes the law into his own hands."

"Somebody's got to," said Gantry.

"Do not overstep your bounds, suh," advised Cravens gravely. "I graduated at the top of my class at the University of Virginia, and I am familiar with the law."

Gantry remembered hearing, somewhere, that familiarity bred contempt.

"I haven't read a bunch of books on the subject, Judge," he said, "but I know what the law is, same as you. It's what every man knows in his heart is right. Come on, Mercy. Let's go."

Holstering the Colt, he picked up the Henry repeater and escorted Mercy out of the jail.

Pausing on the boardwalk, he took a slow and thorough survey of the street. The mob was gone. In its place were small groups of men, positioned up and down the street. Gantry felt their stares, and their animosity.

Across the street stood one of Tenaha's few two-story structures, the Evangeline Hotel. He bent his steps that way, hoping he could get a room overlooking the jail. Clearly Joshua Thorn had been talking straight about the sheriff of Tenaha being a Foley partisan. But Judge Cravens had, more or less, acknowledged his authority—federal authority—and Gantry didn't think the judge would let Hoag go so far as to release the Daggetts. Still, it wouldn't hurt to have a front room at the Evangeline, from whence he could observe the hoosegow comings and goings. The Daggetts had a lot of friends, some of whom might take a notion to break them out, and it was highly unlikely Linus Hoag would put up much resistance.

Reaching the hotel's boardwalk, he remembered Mercy, and turned to find she had followed in his wake.

"You better go on," he said. "I told you it wasn't safe hanging around me."

"But . . . aren't I gonna be your witness, mister?"

"No. You've done enough, and I'm obliged. But you're free of the Daggetts now." He dug into a pocket, found a ten-dollar gold piece and held it out to her. "This'll get you started."

She reached out. Instead of taking the hard money, she grabbed his wrist.

"I ain't got nowhere to go," she whispered.

Gantry tried to pull gently free, cursing himself for being a royal fool. He'd known it was a mistake bringing Mercy along. But what could he do? Leave her out on the street? He looked about him, at the dark figures lurking in night shadow, and realized he could not.

"All right," he said, gruffly, disgusted with himself. "I'll get you a room for the night. Tomorrow we'll figure out what to do with you."

For the first time he saw her smile, and it astonished him, because when she smiled, she was downright pretty.

Chapter Fifteen

The Evangeline's desk clerk had been forewarned. He declared, in a high-pitched voice, nervously cleaning his see-betters with a handkerchief, that there were no vacancies. The skeleton keys hanging from a board on the wall behind the counter contradicted this claim. Gantry signed the register for both himself and Mercy, paid in advance, two dollars a room, and went around the counter to select two keys.

"Second floor, up front," he said. "Which ones?"

Fearing physical damage at the hands of the rough-looking six-foot-six lawman, the clerk cringed.

"You don't want me to have to come back down here," said Gantry, reaching for one of the keys.

"Not that one!" shrieked the clerk. "Numbers 5 and 6, sir."

Gantry took the keys so numbered. "I'd be obliged for water, soap, and a razor."

"Fresh water in the room, sir. I'll see to the rest."

Escorting Mercy to her room, and telling her to keep the door locked at all times, Gantry went to his own room, next to hers. Before lighting a lamp, he spent a few minutes at the window, studying the street and the jail across from the hotel. The street was dark and quiet. Satisfied, he closed the heavy velveteen drapes and lighted a camphene lamp.

A little while later, the clerk arrived with shaving accouterments. Gantry was about finished scraping beard stubble off his face when a knock on the door made him jump. He nicked himself with the straight razor, grimaced at his reflection in the cheap oval mirror hanging on the wall above the dresser. Blood turned to pink the lather on his throat. He was tired, his nerves on edge.

He whipped the door open and stuck the Colt Dragoon in the face of the man standing in the hall, fist raised to knock a second time.

The man looked coolly at the long barrel of the horse pistol an inch from the tip of his nose.

"I seem to have disturbed you."

Gantry spotted the black leather grip in the man's right hand.

"Dr. Treadgold?"

"Yes. Marshal Gantry, I presume."

Gantry lowered the revolver. "Sorry. I thought you might be somebody else."

"I'm glad I wasn't."

Smiling faintly, Treadgold slipped past into the room. Gantry checked the hall, closed the door, and turned the key in the lock.

"Wise precaution, that," said Treadgold. "I refer to the key in the lock. There is a master key."

"Thanks."

"I do what I can to prevent bloodshed. As it is, God knows, I do not want for business."

"Joshua Thorn?"

"In my care. That is what I've come to relay to you. As soon as we heard of your arrival, Mrs. Thorn asked me to find you."

"How is he?"

"A nasty bump on the head. Took quite a few stitches. Otherwise he is well. The Thorns are a hardy breed. Not even four years of easy living back East could soften a tough specimen like Joshua."

"Sounds like you're a friend to the Thorns."

"An acquaintance," said Treadgold ambiguously. He put the grip on the bed and strolled to the window. Parting the drapes, he peered out at the night. He was a trim and handsome man in his thirties, well-dressed in broadcloth, dark brown hair and mustache well-groomed. Highly educated, with an air of polished refinement—not what Gantry had expected in a country doctor serving a backwoods town.

"I wouldn't stick my neck out, if I were you," advised Gantry. "Reckon they know what room I'm in by now. They might try a little target practice."

"At least you do not underestimate the danger you are in." Treadgold turned from the window, taking a pocket flask from his coat. "Brandy?"

"No thanks."

"For medicinal purposes only," joked Treadgold, taking a sip. "I hear you brought in two of the Daggetts."

"Yep. Buried a third."

"Mrs. Thorn informed me of the ambush on the Trammel Trace. Luke Foley escaped?"

Gantry nodded.

"A shame."

"I'll get him back."

"The Foley place is an armed camp. Alone, you stand no chance."

"You've been there?"

"I have. You might say I was fetched on several occasions to treat various members of the clan—gunshot wounds in every instance, I might add. Not to say that is surprising."

"Then you can tell me how to get there. You could take me."

"No, I'm afraid I cannot."

"I didn't take you for a Foley man."

"I don't take sides," said Treadgold severely. "My personal feelings do not count. Mine is a sacred oath, to save lives. I shall not be a party to the taking of them. Whether my patients are good men or bad does not enter into the equation with me. I hope you will respect that, Marshal."

"I guess I'll have to."

Treadgold's dapper smile returned. "I must urge you to give up the idea of going after Luke Foley."

"I also took an oath."

Treadgold nodded. He took a long look around the room. His gaze came to rest on the Henry repeater lying on the bed.

"Speaking of oaths, perhaps I should acquaint you with the Foleys, and the many others in the Redlands like them."

Gantry went back to shaving. "Go ahead, Doctor.

100

The Bible says 'know thine enemy.'"

"Most of the men around here fought for the Confederacy. It's safe to say the majority of them never surrendered. Reconstruction was salt in the wound. It bred tremendous resentment all across the South."

"I know. I was around then."

"You fought in the war?"

"Yeah. I fought Indians. When the United States Army pulled out of Texas, the Comanches thought they could have a field day."

"You didn't fight for the Confederacy?"

"I fought for Texas. For the women and children left out on the plains, while their menfolk went off to die for fine ideals."

"You didn't believe in the Cause, I take it."

"Let's just say I agreed with Sam Houston, that it wasn't a fight Texas needed to buy into."

"I see." Treadgold indulged in another sip of brandy. "Well, as you probably know, after the war a great many Southerners came west. They refused to submit to what they believed to be Yankee tyranny. Some went to Mexico."

Gantry nodded. Diehard Rebels had made a mass exodus to a Confederate colony in Carlota, under the auspices of Emperor Maximilian, then the ruler of Mexico. High-ranking officers like Jo Shelby, Jubal Early, Sterling Price, and Edmund Kirby Smith had led small bands of graycoat soldiers across the Rio Grande. Civilians followed, a steady stream of migrants. Some dreamed of an alliance with the French of Napoleon III to invade Texas and continue the war with the Yankees. Others had hoped to build a new Confederacy in Latin America.

"Quite a few remained in the Redlands," continued Treadgold. "For years after the war, Rebel guerrillas used these woodlands as a base of operations to strike at Federal Occupation forces. As you may have noticed, this is ideal outlaw country. Small armies can vanish without trace into these forests."

"I can imagine."

"The two oldest Foley boys, Matt and Mark, fought for the South. In Missouri, for the most part. Bloody Bill's partisan rangers. Side by side with the likes of Jesse James. Were you aware of that?"

"No."

"The Foley boys refused to take the amnesty oath. They weren't alone. A lot of Southern soldiers resented Federal efforts to force ex-Confederates to swear allegiance to the Stars and Stripes. They'd fought for their homeland; they didn't consider themselves traitors."

Finished with his shave, Gantry washed his face and toweled it dry.

"What's your point, Doctor?"

"The point is, you are a United States Marshal. You uphold federal law. They don't acknowledge federal law in the Redlands. The Foleys and their friends are still at war with the Union, and that makes you the enemy. They have support. Judge Cravens, for instance. He used to be a wealthy Mississippi planter. He owned two plantations, over one hundred slaves. Lost it all to the carpetbaggers. States Rights is still a rallying cry here, Marshal. These people refuse to knuckle under to the Occupation, and they won't knuckle under to you."

"The Foleys are outlaws," said Gantry. "They might claim they're still fighting the Lost Cause, but that's just an excuse, and we both know it."

Treadgold shrugged. "Let it not be said I didn't try to warn you."

"What would you have me do?"

"Go home. Back to your family. Live a while longer."

"I haven't got a family. There's nobody home for me."

Treadgold stared at Gantry a moment, sensing the depth of the man's loneliness, realizing Gantry's heart and soul commitment to his badge and all that the badge symbolized was a result of this loneliness.

"Besides," said Gantry, "When I get Luke Foley to Jefferson, he's going to hang. The Redlands will be better for it. With Luke gone, you might have a few less gunshot wounds to deal with."

"Sadly, it doesn't work that way. Luke Foley dies and his people will go on a rampage. They'll have their vengeance, and they won't be particular about who they take it out on."

"I'm taking Luke Foley in," said Gantry, adamant.

Treadgold sighed and picked up his bag. "Well, I must be going. I've said what I came to say."

Gantry unlocked the door, held it open. Treadgold paused at the threshold.

"Good luck, Marshal," he said, sincerely. "God knows, you'll need it."

Chapter Sixteen

They came for him at dawn.

Gantry snapped awake, rolling off the bed, bringing the Colt Dragoon from under the pillow. He heard the crash of splintered wood as they broke down the door to Mercy's room. He heard her scream, sharply curtailed, a thump, a thud, a man's gruff curse.

They'd picked the wrong room.

He was fully dressed, with the exception of his boots. He couldn't remember the last time he hadn't slept in his clothes. Opting for the weapon more familiar to him, he stuck the pistol in his belt and snatched up the Henry leaning against the wall beside the bed.

Last night he had wedged a chair against the door, under the knob. Now he kicked it aside, turned the key, threw open the door, and stepped out into the hallway.

The corridor was dark. He remembered a lamp burning last night, in a wall bracket at the head of the stairs. The marauders had taken the precaution of snuffing out that lamp. Smoky dawn light in the window at the end of the hall outlined the shapes of two men, ten strides away from Gantry, near Mercy's door.

"Sonuvabitch ain't here!" someone growled. "Wrong room—"

"Big mistake," said Gantry, levering a round into the Henry's chamber, the repeater held at hip level.

The bullet hissed past his head, followed a fraction of a second later by the orange spurt of flame from a gun barrel. Gantry fired, levered, fired again. The three gunshots blended into one peal of gun thunder, trapped in the confines of the hall. One of Gantry's bullets shattered the window, the other smashed into flesh and bone. A sharp grunt, and one of the dark shapes crumpled.

More men boiled out into the hall from Mercy's room. Gantry's finger tightened on the Henry's trigger, then eased off. He saw bare legs pale in the gloom, a hint of yellow hair in the shadow.

"Drop it, I got the girl!" yelled a man hoarsely, the words spilling out fast, running together.

Another bright burst of flame. The bullet chunked into the wall as Gantry darted back into his room.

Cursing under his breath—he'd had a hunch from the get-go that letting Mercy string along spelled trouble—he moved with quick strides to the window. No time for thinking it through; instinct warned him he was dead if they captured him. He couldn't fight back, not with Mercy in the line of fire. Only chance was escape, and the only means of escape was the window. A long jump, but he had to try it.

He didn't get to. As he tore the drapes down and raised the Henry to smash the window, the glass exploded inward. The crackling roar of several rifles fired almost simultaneously from the street below. He spun away from the spray of glass, the angry *spat-spat-spat* of hot lead.

"Take him!"

He spun, glimpsed two men charging through the door, brought the Henry down, and fired. One of the men cried out and fell. Two more took his place. They slammed into Gantry, driving him into the wall. A fist smashed into his chest, another hit below the waist, blasting hot waves of nausea through his body. He struck downward across one man's neck with his arm; threw his knee up into another's face.

Two more men hurled themselves into the fray. A gun barrel caught him on the cheekbone, almost knocking him out. Hot blood streamed down his face. A hand clawed at his eyes. He bit down savagely on the fleshy part between thumb and forefinger. The man loosed a guttural scream. Gantry's mouth was instantly filled with warm, salty blood. The Henry was wrenched out of his grasp. Fists and gun barrels rained down on him. The hand on his face was gone. He spat out a fragment of flesh and a lot of blood, groped for the Colt in his belt, was dismayed to find it gone. Too bad, he thought. He could have taken a couple more with him. He began to punch, his big iron-hard fists causing a lot of damage. He was determined to cause as much as he could before he went down.

Someone hooked his leg, threw him off balance. He fell, and they fell on top of him, punching and pistol-whipping and cursing him. Inch by inch, blow by blow, he weakened, fighting now most of all against unconsciousness, sure that this time he would be unconscious forever, but curiously untroubled by the prospect. He did not beg for life—not even life was worth begging for.

"Goddamn you!" railed one of the men, so close to his face that Gantry could smell the reek of liquor on his breath. He saw a glimmer of light on a raised gun barrel.

"Same to you," he hissed through clenched teeth, straining against the weight of his enemies, watching with curious detachment the gun barrel sweep down. He heard a loud brittle noise, saw a flash of white light, and was gone.

He came to when Linus Hoag dumped a bucket of water on his head.

"Get up, you sorry sonuvabitch."

Gantry tried to get his bearings. He was lying on his back, in a cell. His hands were tied behind his back. One of his eyes was swollen shut. He hurt all over. Too many pains to catalog, no way to tell how much harm had been inflicted on him. He was surprised to find himself still among the living.

"I said get the hell up!" shouted Hoag, grabbing him by the front of his shirt and hauling him up into a sitting position. That was as far as Hoag could haul Gantry's two hundred pounds of muscle and hard grit.

Disgusted, Hoag gestured curtly, and two men entered the cell and roughly got Gantry to his feet.

107

They were about to take him out when Hoag stopped them.

"Just a minute, boys."

Hoag stepped around in front of Gantry, real close.

"You think you're better than me, don't you?"

"Doesn't take much," mumbled Gantry.

Hoag punched him in the mouth. Gantry sagged. The two men held him up, and Hoag hit him once more for good measure.

"What do you think about that, Marshal?" sneered Hoag.

Gantry spat a mouthful of blood and tooth fragments into the Tenaha sheriff's face.

Hoag reeled away, came back snarling hate and pounding his fists into Gantry's midsection. Any other time and Gantry would scarcely have felt the fat little man's blows. This time, though, his whole body was unbelievably sore, and the punches hurt. He doubled over, but the men on either side of him yanked him upright, and Hoag kept hitting. Gantry endured the pain without a sound.

After a while Hoag was winded, his wrath spent. He stepped back, rubbing first one set of knuckles and then the other, and nodded curtly.

"Take this piece of United States scum the hell out of my jail."

They dragged him across the office. Gantry got his feet under him, walking by sheer force of will. Fierce pride kept him going now, and little else. But it was enough for him. He wouldn't let them haul him out like a sack of grain.

It was full daylight now. The brightness made him flinch. The street held twenty, maybe thirty men

108

The crowd kicked up a ruckus when they saw him. Some cut loose with rebel yells. Others shouted curses and obscenities at him. A few were able to articulate the intentions of the whole, yelling for his blood.

"Hang him!"

"Yeah, string the bastard up!"

"Leave him hangin' for crowbait!"

Several ropes, nooses built, were held aloft. *They can only kill you once,* thought Gantry. Regarding ways to die, he had no preference. The means did not matter as much as the way you faced it. Death wasn't so hard. Anticipating death was the hardest part. So one could argue that life was worse than death, because you went through life with the constant knowledge that you were going to die.

A man mounted the boardwalk, grabbing at him, trying to pull him into the mob. Hoag appeared to shove the man back into the others. The Tenaha sheriff toted a sawed-off shotgun now; he fired one barrel skyward to get everyone's attention. It worked magnificently. When a scattergun spoke, people tended to listen. The crowd settled down in a heartbeat.

"What's wrong with you boys?" yelled Hoag.

"Give him to us, Linus!"

"We'll show 'em what happens when they come in here and muddy up our water."

"He killed Jesse Daggett, and he's gotta pay."

"Blood for blood, Sheriff!"

Hoag raised the shotgun again, but he didn't have to fire off that second load.

"You boys are gonna give Marshal Gantry the

109

wrong idea," said Hoag, flashing a yellow, wolfish grin. "We gotta show him we ain't entirely uncivilized down here." Hoag turned the grin on Gantry. "He's gonna pay, all right. Don't fret on that score. But we're gonna do it nice and legal. Just the way the Marshal would want it. Now bring him!"

Hoag led the way, bulling through the mob. The two men with a grip on Gantry followed. The mob fell in behind, a rough and rowdy procession howling for blood.

Chapter Seventeen

Judge Cravens presided in the Tenaha town hall, grim and severe in his black suit, seated behind a table on the platform at the rear of the long clapboard building. Before and below him were two more tables. Behind these stood a low railing, and beyond the railing two rows of benches.

Looking out over the hall, Cravens decided the entire town was present, milling around beyond the railing, everyone talking at once, some with voices raised in anger. Morning sun slanted through tall narrow windows, yellow shafts of light piercing a haze of dust and smoke.

Hoag had just delivered Gantry, and the defendant's arrival had stirred up the crowd. The marshal sat slumped in a chair at one of the tables, with Hoag standing behind him, gloating. Gantry's clothes were torn and bloody. His face was an unholy mess.

The judge wielded his gavel, hammering for order. He was not heard above the din. With a sigh, he pulled a pistol from beneath his coat and fired a round into the ceiling. The crowd settled down.

"Everybody sit!" he yelled, glowering ferociously. "This court will come to order."

There was general compliance. A baby was crying somewhere in the back. Women and children had come to witness the proceedings. Everyone was expecting a fine show.

"The defendant will rise and state his full name," said Cravens.

Gantry didn't move. Cravens scowled, nodded to Hoag. The sheriff drew his gun, cocked it, and pressed the barrel against Gantry's head.

"Best do as the judge says, hoss."

Gantry still didn't move. His eyes were glued to Cravens. Angry murmurs rippled through the crowd.

"Go ahead and blow his brains out, Linus!" suggested one of the onlookers.

Cravens pounded the table with his gavel.

"Gantry," he said, "you will rise and state your full name for this court, or I will find you in contempt."

"Go ahead," said Gantry. "Because I am."

Hoag laid the barrel of his gun across Gantry's skull. Gantry fell sideways out of his chair. A ragged cheer rose from the crowd, subsiding only when Cravens once again hoisted his pistol.

"Return the defendant to his chair, Sheriff," said Cravens sternly.

Hoag had to enlist the aid of the two men who had escorted Gantry from the jail. Gantry was conscious, but just barely.

"Mr. Gantry, suh," said Cravens, "you are charged

with one count of murder and three counts of attempted murder. How do you plead?"

"Who am I supposed to have murdered?"

"Jesse Daggett."

"That was self-defense."

"So your plea is not guilty."

"Will it make any difference?"

"Do you deny you shot and wounded three men this morning in the Evangeline?"

"They fired at me. I shot back."

"Those men had been deputized by Sheriff Hoag and were there to make a lawful arrest."

"There's nothing lawful about any of this."

"You are mistaken, suh," said Cravens with stiff dignity. "You face grave consequences. Two of the three men you shot this morning are in critical condition. They may well die before this day is done. What say you in your defense?"

"I thought I was a better shot."

Cravens shook his head. "A remark which demonstrates your callous disregard for the lives of others. Do you care so little, I wonder, for your own life?"

Gantry didn't respond. A man stood in the crowd and bellowed, "Hang him, Judge, and be done with it!"

Cravens used the gavel again. "Sit down, suh. We will conduct ourselves like civilized men. Justice will be done, of that you may be sure."

Gantry smiled bitterly. Aside from the fact that he was about to be put to death, he found this farce amusing.

"Now, Mr. Gantry," said Cravens, fixing wire-rimmed spectacles over his ears and consulting papers on the table before him. "I have depositions here from Watt Daggett and his son Bob, given under oath and in my presence, asserting that you trespassed upon their property, shot an unarmed Jesse Daggett to death, and wounded Bob Daggett . . ."

Gantry wasn't listening. He thought about Mercy. What had become of her? She could bear witness to what had actually happened. But he rejected the thought as soon as it occurred to him. In the first place, these people wouldn't listen to her. They'd made up their minds. His death warrant was signed. They were just going through the motions, justifying in their own minds what they were about to do. In the second place, he didn't want her involved. He could only hope she had gotten away.

"For the final time, Mr. Gantry, I give you an opportunity to speak in your defense."

Gantry managed to stand up, kicking the chair away. Hoag jumped, then looked furtively about, hoping no one had noticed. Everyone's attention was focused on Gantry. The hall was suddenly deathly quiet. Even the infant had stopped squalling.

"I never killed a man who wasn't trying to kill me," said Gantry, loud and clear. "I shot Bob Daggett all right—on the Trammel Trace. He and his brother and his father, along with several other men, blew up a bridge, wrecked a stage, and killed the driver. They came within an inch of killing an innocent woman. I tracked the Daggetts. I wanted to bring 'em back alive. Jesse Daggett went for a gun and I killed him. That's the truth of it. Just in case there's anybody in this room interested in truth, which I doubt.

114

"Judge, I reckon you're going to hang me. Well, I advise you not to dally too long. Because if I get half a chance, I'm going to give you and this kangaroo court of yours a taste of some real honest-to-God justice."

"*Fire!*"

The shout came from the rear of the hall. A woman shrieked. Dense black smoke billowed in a back corner.

Instant pandemonium—shouts, oaths, screams. They were all on their feet, pushing and shoving, knocking each other down in their hurry to escape. No one needed to be told a clapboard building would burn like a tinderbox.

"Did you say you wanted half a chance, Marshal?"

Gantry spun around, as did Hoag, and at the same time they saw the man, the only person in the place still sitting. He appeared quite relaxed, seated on the bench directly behind them, arms folded, head down, his hat brim pulled low. When he raised his head, every trace of color drained from Hoag's face.

"Jesus Christ!" choked the Tenaha sheriff. His hand dropped to the butt of the pistol in his holster.

Gantry got a glimpse of a strong stubborn chin, pale blue eyes in a sun-dark face, long yellow hair curling to the shoulders.

The man stood, unfolding his arms, and in so doing brandished a pair of cap-and-ball Remingtons from under his blanket coat. Hoag didn't even clear leather. The Remingtons boomed, the slugs punched Hoag in the chest, lifting the sheriff off his feet and slamming him down on the table. The table gave way and Hoag crashed to the floor.

"Look out!" yelled the man, and swept Gantry aside. A bullet splintered the railing between them. On the platform, Cravens was standing erect with shoulders squared, gun arm locked rigidly, like a duelist on the field of honor. He thumbed the hammer back, but didn't get off a second shot. The man with the Remingtons fired twice more. Cravens shuddered, turned away, took one step, and fell like cut timber.

His killer vaulted the railing with a panther's grace. One of the Remingtons vanished beneath the blanket coat. He whipped a knife out of his boot and sliced the rope that bound Gantry's wrists together.

"Follow me."

The man took a running leap through the nearest window.

Gantry hesitated, but only for a second. A bullet shimmied over his head. He went out the shattered window on the man's heels. His landing outside was less graceful than his guide's. His legs gave out under him, and he ate dirt. Strong hands hauled him up. He was near the end of his rope, needing a boost to get into the bed of a spring wagon.

The man who had shot Hoag and Cravens climbed aboard a prancing red roan, spoke to another man on the spring wagon's seat.

"Where's Zach?"

"Here he comes now."

A third man came running around the corner of the town hall. He leaped aboard another horse, foot scarcely touching stirrup.

"They're too busy fightin' the fire to fight us, Logan," reported Zach, sounding disappointed.

Logan nodded to the man driving the wagon. "Gee 'em up, Cousin Tennally."

"My pleasure, Cousin Thorn."

The wagon jerked into motion as Tennally whipped up the team. Gantry lay flat on his back, too exhausted to keep his eyes open. But when cool fingers tenderly touched his damaged face, they snapped open again.

"Mercy!"

She was bending over him, smiling, her yellow hair like spun gold glistening in the morning sun.

"Rest easy, mister. You're safe now."

Chapter Eighteen

She was the last person he saw prior to passing out, sprawled in the back of a spring wagon racketing out of Tenaha. And she was the first person he saw when he came to.

He was still flat on his back, but on a soft mattress now instead of bouncing painfully on rough wagon boards. She was bending over him, applying a cool wet cloth to his forehead, and she was positively beaming. Now her hair gleamed in lamplight, rather than sun.

His first sensation was a tight constriction around his chest. With his head propped up on pillows, he could look down at the dressing wrapped tightly about him—so tightly that normal breathing was difficult.

Then he realized he was buck naked. True, a sheet and counterpane covered him from the chest down, but the fact remained he was lying in bed without a stitch of clothes on, alone in a room with a member of the opposite sex. Ingredients for keen embarrassment to a man whose life had been practically devoid of intimate contact with persons of the female persuasion.

"Where are my clothes?" he asked, the words etched in panic, by reflex clutching the covers and pulling them closer to his chin.

"I'm not a child anymore, mister," she said, a gentle rebuke.

"No . . . no, you're not." He scolded himself for acting so, and thought it wise to change the subject. Looking about, he saw a small room with walls of chinked log, a solitary window with calico drapes. It was dark outside, full night. He spotted his saddle, longcoat, and rifle on a cedar chest under the window.

"Where am I?"

"Logan Thorn's cabin. We brought you here. Don't you remember?"

"Some."

She, too, looked around the room, suddenly pensive.

"Mr. Thorn says he don't stay in this room no more, not since his wife died. Ain't that sad?"

"Mercy, you look . . . different."

The smile returned—she was shyly pleased he had noticed. Her face was scrubbed clean, her hair washed and brushed out, and she wore a blue-checked gingham dress.

"Mr. Thorn gave me this dress. I didn't want to take it at first. Belonged to his wife. But he insisted. Said I looked pretty as a picture." She looked down at herself with an expression of wonder. "I never wore a dress like this before."

"I'm glad you're okay, Mercy."

"When they went after you, they plumb forgot about me." She touched his face. "They hurt you something fierce, didn't they?"

"I'll be all right."

"After they took you away, I run to the doc's place. He got me a horse and told me to fetch the Thorns. He tried to get into the jail to see you, but they turned him away."

Gantry could hear men talking in the next room. "Who's out there?"

"The Thorns. Doc Treadgold, too. A couple others. I think they're kin to the Thorns. A lady, too. Joshua Thorn's wife. They just finished up supper. You hungry?"

Gantry realized he was famished. He hadn't eaten since the breakfast at Hannah Malone's roadhouse. How long ago? Seemed like a small eternity.

"I could eat a horse, hooves and all."

"I'll fetch something."

"Mercy."

She paused, her hand on the door latch.

"Thanks," he said. "You saved my life."

She gave him a long and unreadable look. He sensed he had not spoken the words she had wanted to hear. He didn't have a clue what the right words might be. But she accepted his gratitude with a nod and slipped out of the room.

Treadgold and Logan Thorn came in a moment later. The dapper doctor took Gantry's pulse—measured against his Ingersoll keywinder—then took a close look at Gantry's good eye, holding it wide open with thumb and forefinger. He held up two fingers and asked Gantry how many fingers he saw. He told the marshal to watch the fingers, and moved his hand left and right, then up and down. Finally he nodded, satisfied.

"You have a hard head, Marshal."

"So I've been told."

"You also have a cracked rib, a sprained ankle, numerous contusions, and abrasions. You lost a couple of teeth. The little finger of your left hand was dislocated."

Gantry raised his left hand. The little finger had been set and then wrapped tightly to the next finger.

"Hope that's not your gun hand, friend," remarked Logan.

"No."

"Didn't have time for introductions back in Tenaha," drawled Logan, with a loose grin. "Name's Logan Thorn."

Gantry's features were grim-set. "Guess I owe you thanks."

"My pleasure."

The cold efficiency of Logan Thorn as he gunned down Hoag and Cravens was vivid in Gantry's mind.

"You were pretty quick to kill back there," he said.

Logan's grin was frozen in place. "They'd have done the same to me, given the chance."

"But you didn't give them one. Hoag didn't have a snowball's chance in hell against you."

"I reckon you're more fair-minded than me," said Logan, with glacial courtesy. "That must be why I'm standing here fit as a Tennessee fiddle, and you're laid up there beat more than half to death."

Gantry forced a smile. His first impression of

121

Logan Thorn, blazing Remingtons included, was not an especially good one, but he could not dispute the fact that this man had pulled his fat out of the fire.

"Don't mean to sound ungrateful."

"Least you speak your mind. We just see things different, but we're on the same side. I'll go tell Joshua you're awake. He's got a damfool notion and wants to parlay with you."

When the door had closed behind Logan, Treadgold said, "There is good and bad in every man, and it is sometimes difficult to tell which has the upper hand with Logan. Life has knocked him down on occasion, and each time he gets back up, he is a little the worse for wear."

"Obliged for your help, Doc. Should be some money in my saddlebags . . ."

"On the house, Marshal. Let's call it a small contribution to law and order. Though I must admit that since your arrival here lawlessness and disorder seem to prevail."

"What about the men I shot in the hotel?"

"Two should survive. The third died this morning." Treadgold shrugged. "I have a feeling I should prepare myself for more of the same."

"You going to tell me to go home again?"

"It's too late for that, Marshal."

Gantry nodded.

"If you want to thank someone," said Treadgold, "it should be the girl. She had you cleaned up and poulticed before I got here."

Gantry felt his cheeks get hot. "You mean she . . ."

Treadgold chuckled. "You *were* banged up from head to heel, and she seems bound and determined to be the one to do for you. If I may say so, I think she is rather taken with you."

"Get her out of here, Doc, will you? She's in harm's way."

"A team of wild horses couldn't drag her away from your side."

"Damn," muttered Gantry darkly.

Treadgold studied him a moment, speculatively.

"You know, I've often thought the heart takes longest to heal."

"What is that supposed to mean?"

Treadgold opened his mouth to say something, changed his mind, and shook his head. "Nothing. Merely an observation."

Logan returned, followed by Joshua Thorn and Laura. Joshua's head was bandaged. He appeared happy to see Gantry above snakes. His wife looked distraught.

"I told you the only law in Tenaha was Foley law," said Joshua.

"Ain't no law period, anymore," said Logan.

"That's precisely what I wish to discuss with you, Marshal," said Joshua. "It is my understanding that you possess the authority to appoint a sheriff pro tem, until such time as fair elections can be conducted. I'm applying for the job."

"He sure does talk fancified now," said Logan, grinning. "Sounds like a feller who's been four years back East, don't he? Too fancy-talking to be a sheriff."

"I can handle it."

"Little brother, you'd have to learn to shoot straighter to handle it." Logan glanced at Gantry.

"He told me about running into Luke Foley at the Malone house. Damn shame I wasn't there. Then we'd have one less Foley to worry about. But Joshua didn't see fit to send word and let us know when he was coming."

"Tenaha needs a sheriff, Marshal," said Joshua resolutely. "If you don't appoint one, Ma Foley will."

"I don't know, Joshua," said Treadgold, dubious. "The town is full to the rafters with ruffians and deadbeats, and most of them side with the Foleys. They like the way the Foleys wreak havoc on the railroads and the banks, most of which are still run by Union men. Your wearing a badge wouldn't sit well with them, I'm afraid."

"Don't do it, Joshua," begged Laura. "They'll kill you for sure."

"Marshal, I can do the job."

"Forget it," said Gantry. "I want all of you to stay out of it."

"Be reasonable," urged Joshua. "You can't take them all on by yourself. You're a marked man. You killed Jesse Daggett."

"I said no."

Joshua was set to argue the point, but Mercy arrived with a bowl of chicken broth. She set this on the table by the bed and turned on them, hands on hips. Gantry did not fail to notice the bright intense way Logan watched her.

"He needs rest and quiet," she said sharply, "so I think you all best dust out of here before I lose my temper."

"Marshal, you're one lucky cuss," grinned Logan, and pulled his brother out of the room.

Treadgold was the last one out. "I'll be by tomorrow to check on you." He winked at Mercy. "Take good care of him. He'll want to get up tomorrow. Don't let him. Just don't give him his clothes. I wager that will keep him under the covers."

When he was gone, Mercy sat on the edge of the bed and picked up the bowl. "Doc says this is all you should have tonight."

"I can feed myself," he said curtly. Too curtly.

Her expression went blank. She put the bowl back on the table, went to a chair in the corner.

Gantry sat up, wincing at a sudden stab of pain in his chest. He modestly arranged the covers. He sipped a few spoonfuls of broth.

"I made it myself," she said, watching his every move.

Gantry forced himself to take a little more. She sat there, hands clasped in her lap, staring at him.

"Good," he said.

"I'm not a very good cook," she admitted. "But then you're not a very good liar, mister. Does that make us even?"

He put the bowl on the table and stared right back at her.

"Mercy."

"Yes?"

"You beat all I ever saw."

She smiled.

He couldn't help himself. He had to smile back.

Chapter Nineteen

As Treadgold had anticipated, Gantry was not the kind of man who would abide bed rest. The next day he expressed in no uncertain terms his intention to get up and about. To his surprise, Mercy brought him his mended clothes.

The lesser pains had subsided. Mercy had applied a bread and milk poultice to his injured eye. By morning the swelling was greatly reduced, and he could see with that eye again. She put turpentine mixed with lard on some of his other bruises and aches, and the concoction worked wonders.

But as the lesser pains went away, the pain in his chest from the cracked rib became correspondingly more severe. He could not draw a deep breath without almost passing out. He had a hell of a time just pulling on his boots. Gantry resigned himself to the fact that the rib would be slow to heal. He knew it would do so at a more rapid pace if he exercised some self-discipline and stayed in bed. But he just couldn't do it. The little room was suffocating him.

He made it as far as the front porch, Mercy hovering near him, ready to help him if he faltered, though he doubted she weighed in at a hundred pounds soaking wet. Settling with a disgusted sigh into a rocking chair, he contented himself with studying the lay of the land.

The morning was bright and refreshingly cool. A small horseshoe valley, hemmed in by green pine-cloaked hills, lay before him. A quarter-mile north stood another cabin with its attendant outbuildings, and near it he spotted two men plowing a field. Time for planting. A creek purled in a steep ravine behind the cabins, at the foot of the western hills, and the banks of the ravine were thick with passion vine and wild roses. A gentle breeze carried the fragrance of wood smoke and wildflowers.

A while later Joshua and Laura came over from the other cabin. While Laura and Mercy went inside to prepare the midday meal, Joshua joined Gantry on the porch.

"What do you think of our little valley, Marshal?"

"It'll do."

"My father thought so when he first laid eyes on it. He was a young man with a new bride, and he came for the free land the Republic of Texas was offering emigrants forty years ago. He got a certificate for over twelve hundred acres just for the asking. Land was the only thing Texas had to offer back then. But it is a handsome land. I believe I will build my home yonder. I was born in this valley. I want my sons to be also. This was my father's cabin. Logan's now. That one over there is Zach's. He's been good enough to give it over to Laura and me until we can raise our

127

own. A sacrifice, as he must now bunk with Logan."
Joshua smiled. "What do you think of my wild and
woolly older brother, Marshal?"

"Jury's still out."

"Logan has a wild streak. Always has. When he
heard our father bragging on his old friend Jim
Bowie, and how Bowie used to wrestle alligators for
sport, Logan went off and tried it himself. Picked the
biggest gator in the Redlands. Killed it, too. Brought
the skin back to Father."

"Somehow that doesn't surprise me."

"Father's death hit Logan the hardest. Odd, that,
as Father seemed to favor me and Zach. He used to say
I was the smartest. He wanted me to get an education.
Said I could be anything I wanted to be. Lawyer,
businessman, even governor. And Zach was the baby.
Logan got left out. It embarrassed me. I looked up to
Logan, but Father always looked down on him. I
once overheard Father say that Logan reminded him
too much of himself. Like that was supposed to
explain why he was so hard on Logan. I think Logan
was constantly trying to prove himself to Father."

Gantry said nothing. Joshua gave him a curious
sidelong glance.

"What about your folks?"

"Dead."

"What did your father do?"

"He was a lawman."

"So you followed in his footsteps."

"You could say that."

Gantry was terse. Joshua could tell this was a
subject he did not care to discuss.

"Got a family?"

128

"No."

"That girl Mercy has eyes for you."

Gantry fired him a dark look, then stood, wincing and stepped to the edge of the porch. He leaned heavily against a post and gazed across the bottomland.

"She'll get over it," he said.

"Think so?"

"She'll have to."

"I didn't think I'd ever get hitched, either. Didn't want to give up my freedom." Joshua shook his head, grinning. "Now that I've found Laura, I see how misguided I was."

"It isn't like that with me."

"Mercy seems like a fine person."

"I got her out of a bad situation. That's why she sticks to me. Like I said, she'll get over it."

"You don't cut slack for anybody, do you?"

Gantry turned, his expression intense.

"No, I don't. My father did. That was his mistake. A young gunslinging punk who called himself Kid Spence. My father walked him down, humbled him in front of the whole town. He should have shot to kill when Kid Spence went for his gun. But he disarmed the Kid instead. A few days later, Spence slipped into our house. Grabbed my mother and put a gun to her head. I was seven years old at the time. He told my father to drop his gun, or he'd blow her head off. My father dropped his gun. Kid Spence shot him dead. Then he killed my mother."

"Christ."

"I learned two things that day. One, never cut anybody any slack. Two, never care so much for someone that it makes you vulnerable. It's a chink in a lawman's armor. A weakness that men will use against you, if they get the chance. Those are two rules I live by, and they're the reason I'm still alive."

"There are other lines of work."

"Not for me," replied Gantry, resuming his bleak survey of the valley. "Not as long as there are people like Kid Spence walking this earth."

For a good five minutes not a word passed between them.

"That's why you won't let me help, isn't it?" asked Joshua. "Not because I lost my head and tried to shoot Luke Foley. But because I've got a wife, and you think they might use that against me."

"Maybe."

"This is our fight, too."

"With you it's no fight. It's feud."

"We have a shooting war on our hands, Gantry," snapped Joshua, temper flaring. "I told you before. Long as the Foleys run loose, my wife isn't safe. I want her to be safe, and my children, too. Whether I stay clear of it or not won't make a damn bit of difference. They'll come gunning for me. You started it, bringing Luke Foley through here in irons. A Daggett is gone under, and before you're done a couple more members of the Foley clan will be six feet deep, and then, after they've filled you full of lead, they'll start on the Thorns. The sides have already been drawn. War's been declared since the Foleys and the Daggetts blew that bridge. So I'm going to fight. I've got to. And you can't stop me."

Mercy came out on the porch. She went to the iron triangle hanging from the porch rafters by a rope and

130

rang it to summon Logan and Zach from the field. Impassive, she gave Gantry a long look, her violet eyes unblinking behind their veil of yellow hair. Gantry wondered how much of the conversation she had overheard.

"You're just one man, mister," she said softly. "There's only so much one man can do. Even a man like you."

She went back inside.

Gantry thought it over. He thought long and hard. Logan and Zach arrived, washed up, and they all went in to sit down to table. Fried ham, red gravy, radishes and wild onions, hot biscuits and coffee—just the smell of these vittles made Gantry delirious from hunger. After Joshua said grace, Mercy passed the platter of ham to Gantry.

"What, no broth?" he asked.

"No broth. You're going to need your strength."

Gantry looked around the table. The Thorn boys were watching him.

"I reckon we all will," he said.

Logan grinned like a loafer wolf.

Chapter Twenty

Treadgold had been through the Big Cypress Swamp on his way to the Foley place ten times before. Nonetheless, he was grateful to have a guide. Even a guide like Jestro.

Jestro and the swamp were much alike, mused Treadgold. The swamp and Jestro belonged together, deserved one another. They were both quiet and deadly. Jestro never smiled. The sun never pierced the thick green canopy of interlaced branches overhead. Jestro rarely spoke, and when he did it was usually something vulgar or unpleasant. A breathless hush reigned in the swamp, broken only by the grunting of bull alligators, the slither of cottonmouths in the rank marsh grass, the whine of mosquitoes—skeeters big enough, it was said, they could pick their teeth with the spokes of wagon wheels. Jestro was dirty and sour-smelling even at a distance—which Treadgold faithfully kept. The swamp reeked of death, disease, and decay.

Their horses splashed through murky water, sometimes hock-deep, sometimes deep enough that stirrups skimmed the unctuous surface. The swamp seemed to go on forever in every direction. Tall cypress trees draped with Spanish moss, grassy hillocks, still and scummy pools, a misty half-light obscuring the distance in a shadowy eternal gloom.

Treadgold consulted his keywinder. It was three o'clock. They'd been traveling through the Big Cypress for over an hour, and so he surmised they were very nearly to their destination. But he could not distinguish this stretch of swamp from that which they had negotiated an hour ago. For this reason—certainly no other—he was glad to have Jestro leading the way. Treadgold was not at all sure he could have come this far on his own without becoming hopelessly lost. Maybe . . . but maybes were often fatal in a Redlands swamp. Quicksand and gator holes lurked beneath the surface of this putrid water. There were certain routes one had to stick to. Routes only a select few were sure of. Jestro was sure. His first breath of air had reeked of Big Cypress stench.

Ahead, Jestro rode slumped in the saddle, a shotgun canted across the fork of his hull. Suddenly his spine straightened, the shotgun moved slightly, and Treadgold braced himself for what swiftly followed: the boom of the ten-gauge. A geyser of water thirty feet to their right drew Treadgold's attention, and he glimpsed the thrashing brown black body of a snake in its death throes.

"Goddamn cottonmouth," muttered Jestro dully, breaking open the shotgun, plucking out the spent shell, taking a fresh one from a loop of the bandolier across his bare and brawny chest, and loading up. He did not glance over his shoulder at

Treadgold. He never did. By all appearances, he did not care in the slightest if the doctor was still or ever with him. Treadgold reasoned that of course Jestro *did* care—Ma Foley had dispatched Jestro to Tenaha to fetch the doctor, and everyone knew that failure to do Ma Foley's bidding resulted in fearful repercussions.

Jestro killed every single snake he came across. This had been his sixth cottonmouth victim today. It wasn't that Jestro despised snakes in particular. He just liked to kill things. Cottonmouths were the most numerous targets available. Alligators and snapping turtles were elusive creatures. Cottonmouths were aggressive. The splashing agitation of the water created by the passage of man or beast drew them like iron filings to a magnet.

As the sound of the shotgun blast rolled away, hounds began to bark and bay from somewhere up ahead. Treadgold was only marginally relieved to know his trek through the swamp with Jestro was reaching its conclusion, because it brought him now into the devil's den. A place no decent man concerned for his own well-being felt comfortable.

The Foley cabin stood on a tongue of dry land, surrounded on three sides by marsh. The double cabin, with dogtrot centerpiece, had been added to in a slipshod fashion. It was a rambling unattractive structure of gray weathered wood and cypress shakes. A couple of picket pens held horses. Another contained hogs as large as a full-grown man. A shed, a smokehouse, and several lean-tos augmented the clutter.

As Treadgold and his guide drew near, two hounds came off the porch with such ferocity that the doctor checked his mount. They were mixed breeds, Ma Foley's pets. He'd been told they were mankillers, that only Ma and her sons could handle them. He didn't know if this was true, and he didn't want to know. They were ugly beasts, all fang and sinew. They were also, thank God, on stout lengths of rope, and when the hard-twist sang rigid, they were jerked off their feet and went into a snarling snapping frenzy that subsided only when a man stepped out of the cabin and yelled at them to shut the hell up. The hounds sat on quivering haunches, tongues lolling, and did not take their eyes off Treadgold.

The man came out to greet Jestro and the doctor. He was the oldest Foley boy, Matt. In Treadgold's opinion, John was crazy, Luke was wild, Mark was mean, and Matt was all three things. Matt was thin and wiry, like all the brothers with the exception of Mark. His hair was rust red, his eyes gray as the barrel of a gun.

"Howdy, Jestro. See you found the doc."

"Not all I found," muttered Jestro, dismounting.

"Spit it out."

"Only want to say it once," replied Jestro. Treadgold wasn't sure if he was too mean in his own right, or simply too stupid, to be leery of Matt Foley. "Where's Ma?"

"Paris, France, at the opera. Where the hell do you think?"

Jestro trudged to the cabin, dragging his horse along, tying rein leather to a porch upright.

"How's business, Doc?" asked Matt.

"It's been picking up. Who's hurt this time?"

"It's Luke. That damn lawman shot him. The wound's festerin'. And Ma's been feeling poorly of late."

135

It was a wonder, thought Treadgold, that she was still alive. He dismounted, untied his medical grip from the saddle, and, steeling himself, stepped into the cabin.

The room was dark and rank. Treadgold paused just across the threshold, letting his eyes adjust to the deep gloom of the place. Jestro had his back to him and was talking.

"They done took over the town, Ma. They . . ."

A cackling laugh deteriorated into a coughing fit. The hacking was followed by labored wheezing, a sound resembling that made by a blacksmith's leather bellows.

"Ain't nothin' bullets won't set right," came a deep raspy voice. "Step aside, now. That you, Doc?"

Jestro complied, and Treadgold saw Ma Foley, sitting in a corner. No ordinary chair would accommodate her. A wagon seat, set on stumps and supported by the wall, barely managed. She was obscenely fat. Her skin was mottled and yellowish gray, with the texture of parchment. The calico dress she wore had enough fabric in it, he decided, to cover the topsail of a clipper ship. She had one bare foot propped up on a three-legged stool. Her feet were absurdly small for one so obese.

Treadgold figured Ma Foley was just too ornery to die. He mentally inventoried those of her ailments he had been able to diagnose. She had jaundice; the color of her skin and the yellow taint of the whites of her eyes were the physical symptoms of an excess of bile pigments in her blood. She suffered from gout and could scarcely get about; a cane and a sturdy crutch leaned against the wall within her reach. Her hands were twisted arthritic claws. The lens of her right eye was covered with the milky opacity of a cataract. Recurrent bouts of malaria he could treat with quinine, but he suspected that her heart and kidneys were diseased, and that was what eventually would kill her.

Every time he laid eyes on Ma Foley, Treadgold remembered being told as a child—he could not recall the exact circumstances—that if a person became vile and perverted in his heart, ultimately this depravity would corrupt the physical body. This notion had been one of those childish superstitions he had put aside as he matured. But ever since meeting Ma Foley, he had begun to wonder if there wasn't something to it, after all.

Ma Foley's piggish, yellow-tinged eyes crinkled. The flaccid folds of her face quivered and moved; yellow teeth in dark red gums appeared as she leered at Treadgold.

"Doc, you handsome devil you. Iffen I was ten years younger, I'd get us a bottle and a blanket and we'd have us a good ol' goddamn time."

Treadgold forced a smile, blinked as a rivulet of sweat snaked down his forehead and into his eye. He was afraid of Ma Foley. The fact that she was obviously taken with him did nothing to make him less so.

"Hello, Mrs. Foley. I hear—"

She cackled, and the wagon seat creaked complaint as three hundred pounds of blubber shook with laughter.

"*Mrs.* Foley, he says. A goddamn gentleman, eh, boys?"

Treadgold glanced around the room. Matt was leaning in the doorway, smiling lazily, like he really didn't feel like it. Mark sat at the table playing solitaire. The biggest of the brothers, his was a surly demeanor, with a disposition to match. He spared Treadgold a flinty look and did not smile. A cigarette dangled from his mouth.

"Where's John?" asked Treadgold.

"Sent him over to warn the Daggetts," said Ma Foley, wheezing again. "They don't know that lawman is still above snakes."

Treadgold wasn't surprised Ma Foley knew this. She was kept informed of everything that went on in Shelby County.

"I hear Luke needs attention," he said, hoping to avoid the subject of Marshal Gantry. "Where is he?"

"T'other room. But 'fore you see to him, Doc, I want to ask you a little question. I want to know how come you sent that yeller-haired bitch of Watt's after the Thorns, so's they could save that badge-toter from the rope? On account of that, Judge Cravens and Linus Hoag are feedin' the worms. How come you done such a thing, Doc?"

Mark Foley violently threw his pasteboards down and pulled a knife. The belduque looked about three feet long to Treadgold.

"Yeah, sawbones, that really burned Ma's powder. Personally, it makes me no difference. That lawman shot my little brother, and I'd just as soon cut him up into pieces of bloody meat myself." Mark stood and took a menacing step toward Treadgold. "Mebbe I ought to practice on you first."

Chapter Twenty-One

"Put that pigsticker away," rasped Ma Foley.

Mark spun away from Treadgold and drove the knife into the table. Glowering spitefully at the doctor, he sat down to his cards.

"My son is a fractious fool, Doc, and I apologize," said Ma.

Treadgold found himself as angry as he was scared.

"I do what I must to keep people alive. That's my job. I try not to take sides. I leave the right and wrong of a thing to others. But don't push me."

"Why, Doc, you got more backbone than I give you credit for. So tell me what you think about this Marshal?"

"He's just a man. Better than some, worse than others."

Ma Foley snorted. "A man from the ground up, sounds like to me. After all, he walked right in on the Daggetts, killed Jesse, and hauled Watt and his boy into town against their will. No ordinary run-of-the-mill man could pull that off."

"Like to see him try it on Foleys, 'stead of Daggetts," growled Mark.

"Don't be talkin' down your kin," reprimanded Ma.

"All I'm sayin' is, you let me ride into Tenaha, and I'll prove this Gantry feller can die easy as any other man."

Ma Foley turned her attention back on Jestro.

"You say he took over the town? What do you mean, zackly?"

"What I said. He rode in yesterday with the Thorns backin' him, and them all armed to the teeth. First thing he done was go to the jail and throw Rike Bartell out on his ear."

"I told you Rike couldn't hold onto that sheriff's badge," said Mark. "I'd swear he's first cousin to Moses Rose. He ain't got the guts God gave a jackrabbit."

Treadgold knew Rike Bartell as a shiftless barfly who talked a good game, but made himself scarce as hen's teeth when the going got rough. First cousin to Moses Rose was a Texan's definition of the ultimate coward. Legend had it that a man named Moses Rose was the only defender of the Alamo lacking the intestinal fortitude to step over the line Colonel Travis had drawn in the dirt with his sword. While the other Texans died fighting for freedom, Moses Rose slipped through Santa Anna's lines and high-tailed it.

"I sent word in for Rike to pin Linus Hoag's star on his shirt for a reason," snapped Ma, who did not brook much backtalk. "You don't want a brave man behind a badge, boy. A man puts on a star and

140

sometimes he begins to take himself serious, if he has any grit at all."

"He ain't got a badge no more," announced Jestro. "Gantry took it away from him and moved himself into the jail."

"What else did he do?"

"Sent off a couple telegrams. I got copies of 'em right here, and the answer he got." Jestro took some rolled papers from one of his bandolier loops, handed them to Ma Foley. She gave him a withering look.

"You know I can't read, you idjit."

"I'll read them for you," offered Treadgold.

Gantry's first wire was sent to the U.S. Marshal's Office in Austin, to the attention of Buck Stonecipher.

LUKE FOLEY ESCAPED STOP NO LAW IN SHELBY COUNTY STOP REQUEST PERMISSION TO STAY UNTIL THERE IS STOP

Stonecipher's reply:

USE ANY AND ALL MEANS AT YOUR DISPOSAL STOP DO YOU NEED HELP STOP

To which Gantry had responded:

HAVE ALL THE HELP I NEED STOP

"He means the Thorns, I reckon," remarked Matt.

Ma Foley cast a few choice aspersions on the Thorn name.

"Then he had this printed up and posted all over town," said Jestro, and handed Treadgold a flyer.

"A list of town ordinances," said the doctor.

"Ordinances? What the hell is that in English?" asked Mark.

"Rules."

"Mark don't know what rules are, either," joked Matt.

"Read it," barked Ma Foley.

"'No firearms will be worn in the town limits except by men leaving or entering. All firearms will be checked upon arrival at the hotel, livery, or jail. Firearms may not be discharged in the town limits except on the Fourth of July and New Year's Eve. Horses may not be ridden into any establishment. Persons found on the streets, except those leaving or entering town, after ten o'clock at night, will be arrested.'" Treadgold carefully folded the poster and put it on the table. "In effect, Gantry has declared martial law in Tenaha."

"Marshal law?" Mark grunted. "I say we give him a taste of Foley law."

"Sounds like a curfew to me," said Matt. "I thought the Occupation was over."

Mark glared darkly at Ma. "You gonna let him get away with this? Tenaha's *our* town!"

"Whiskey and women is all you ever go to Tenaha for," replied Ma Foley. "You'll stay clear of town until I say otherwise, hear? You want tongue oil, you can get all the white lightnin' you can hold from Jestro's still. And if it's women you're hankering after, you can head up to Belle Diamond's place."

Treadgold knew Belle Diamond's place was four miles west of Tenaha. The infamous brothel—the most notorious of its kind in the Redlands—had been established after the war in an abandoned plantation house. He'd been there on several occasions, purely business, treating the ailments of various sporting ladies. It was said of Belle Diamond's brothel that if at any given time you found five male patrons within its walls, four would be wanted men.

Mark stared at Ma Foley like he couldn't believe his ears.

"You mean we're gonna knuckle under?"

"More'n one way to skin a cat, boy," replied Ma with a crafty smile. "You go waltzin' into Tenaha, gunnin' for Gantry, you'll be playin' into his hands."

"So what do we do?"

"You don't go into a cave after a wounded bear, that's what you *don't* do. You smoke him out into the open." Ma Foley gave Treadgold a sly sidelong glance. "Jestro, why don't you show the Doc where Luke is?"

Treadgold followed Jestro through a blanket-draped doorway. He figured Ma Foley had a scheme cooked up that boded ill for Gantry, and she didn't want him to be privy to it.

Luke Foley was laid out on a narrow bunk in the cluttered room he shared with the youngest brother, John. Luke had the cold sweats. He was semiconscious, mumbling deliriously. Treadgold could almost smell the infection as he unwrapped the dressing on Luke's leg. He asked Jestro to fetch hot water and clean bandages.

The bullet hole had become inflamed, radiating

red streaks of poison up and down the leg. Matt came in to help Jestro hold Luke down while Treadgold reopened the wound, letting it bleed freely. The blood was streaked with white strings of pus.

"Gantry's gonna pay for this," muttered Matt.

"I hear he cleaned and cauterized the wound," said Treadgold.

"Where'd you hear that?"

Treadgold didn't offer an explanation. Laura Thorn had related to him the events that had occurred at the Malone house and during the subsequent stagecoach ride to Tenaha.

"My guess is he got into swamp water on the way here," he said.

Matt had nothing to say. Treadgold realized he had made up his mind. Gantry was solely responsible for Luke's condition, and Matt wasn't going to change his thinking on that score. For every minute of pain Luke suffered, Matt was committed to giving Gantry an hour's worth. This was the way the Foleys operated.

"He gonna lose the leg?" asked Jestro.

"Too early to say." Treadgold cleansed the wound with carbolic, then applied a salve.

"What's that?"

"Camphor and snake oil," said Treadgold, who had learned long ago to combine the knowledge he had acquired in the medical school at the University of Ohio with home remedies he had discovered on the frontier. He placed a clean dressing on the wound and declared this was all he could do for the time being.

He went back to Ma Foley, found her savoring a smelly cheroot and drinking corn liquor, with which she mixed her quinine. He put the jar of salve on the table.

"How is he?" asked Mark.

"I'll want to come back in a couple of days to check on his condition," said Treadgold. "Meanwhile, the wound needs to be cleaned, and the dressing changed, twice a day at least."

"Got anything for what ails me, Doc?" asked Ma, in a whiny, little girl voice. "I've been a mite down in the mouth. How 'bout some more of them bile beans?"

Treadgold left her a bottle of liver pills. "If you must drink whiskey, you'd do well to mix it with horehound or sarsaparilla."

"You're a good man, Doc, to care so about an ol' witch like me."

"All life is sacred."

"Life is a bitch. And it comes mighty cheap in these parts."

"I'd like to change that attitude," sighed Treadgold, closing up his medical bag.

"Well, you ain't gonna. We're about to have us a little war, Doc."

"Yes," said Treadgold. "I've seen it coming."

"A man in the middle is likely to get caught in a cross fire," said Mark.

Treadgold heard a thinly veiled threat.

"If I'm in the way of a bullet meant for you," he told Mark coldly, "I'll be sure to duck."

Ma Foley busted out laughing. Treadgold could still hear her cackling as he followed Jestro back into the swamp.

Chapter Twenty-Two

A couple days later, Treadgold found Gantry sitting in a chair tipped back on its hind legs against the front wall of the Tenaha jail. The marshal was rolling a smoke. The Henry repeater lay across his lap. He was keeping an eye on the street. It was morning; a bright, clear, cool morning, promising the kind of spring day that made a man feel right with the world, and reminded him to be thankful for the blessing of life.

"Morning, Marshal."

"Doc."

Treadgold gazed along the street, taking the town's pulse. It was surprisingly steady. He hadn't expected Tenaha to submit so meekly to Gantry's law. There had been some head-busting and some men thrown in the hoosegow, but no killings, and for that Treadgold was grateful. This morning Tenaha looked downright docile. Men were sweeping out their places of business. A freight wagon trundled by. The clang of the blacksmith's hammer rang clear as a church bell on the pine-scented air.

"Town looks quiet."

"Looks can be deceiving," said Gantry.

Thumbs hooked in his vest pockets, Treadgold smiled faintly. "You always expect the worst?"

"Where I come from, you can look out across fifty miles of open plains and see nothing but grass and antelope, and the next minute you've got a hundred Comanche warriors in your face."

Gantry scratched a sulfur match to life on his bootheel, lit the roll-your-own.

"How's the rib?"

"Fine."

"If it hurt like the dickens, you wouldn't admit it."

Reticent as usual, Gantry only shrugged. Treadgold saw a single wanted poster on the wall which had once been littered with bounty notices.

"See you got rid of the clutter."

"I figure Hoag put 'em up so that the men could stroll by and see how much they were worth on any given day."

Treadgold stepped closer to read:

$1,000 REWARD

For Information Leading To
The Arrest Of

LUKE FOLEY

WANTED FOR MURDER

"Think that will work?" asked Treadgold.

"No honor among thieves."

"Honor doesn't enter into it. The man who ratted

on Luke Foley wouldn't live long enough to collect the reward."

Gantry smoked his cigarette and observed the street activity.

"This is just a prod," said Treadgold. "A red flag. You're hoping they'll come to you. Well, they won't. You'll remember, I told you Matt and Mark Foley rode with Bloody Bill Anderson in the war. They used guerrilla tactics then, and they'll use them again now. Mark my words, when they strike, it will be where you least expect it."

A rider was coming down the street, leading a horse. It was Zach Thorn, and he was fired up, his face flushed. His words fell over one another.

"Bob Daggett and Johnny Foley are in town."

Gantry stood and flicked a dry I-told-you-so look at Treadgold.

"Logan and me was down at the livery, saddling up," continued Zach, "when the blacksmith told us Bob and Johnny came in a little while ago, and they wouldn't check their guns. Smitty says they were loaded for bear."

"Where are they now?"

"The Buckskin Saloon."

Gantry recognized the horse Zach was leading as one belonging to Logan, and asked the youngest Thorn of his brother's whereabouts.

"He's keeping an eye on the saloon. Sent me down to fetch you."

"It doesn't make sense," said Treadgold. He had a bad feeling—a gut hunch that there was going to be some killing done today. "They're here against Ma Foley's orders."

"Pride goes before the fall," said Gantry.

"Let me talk to them."

"I don't think they came to talk, Doc."

"Give me a chance."

Gantry nodded. It was Zach's presence that made him assent. While he remained in Tenaha and the oldest Tennally brother, Bull, stayed in the valley to watch out for the womenfolk, Logan, Joshua, Zach, and Frank Tennally alternated by twos backing Gantry up in town. Just his luck, thought Gantry now, that he had Zach and Logan with him today. Logan was hotheaded and Zach was too eager. An hour later and they would have been on their way to the Thorn-Tennally homesteads.

Logan was too quick to kill, and that bothered Gantry, but Zach worried him most of all. The youngest Thorn seemed to feel like he had to prove himself—as though killing a Daggett or a Foley was his rite of passage into manhood.

"One thing, Doc," said Gantry. "They can't just ride out. They have to give themselves up."

"You'll put their backs to the wall," protested Treadgold. "You've got to give them a way out."

"No."

"You push too hard," said Treadgold bitterly.

"Five minutes. And the clock just started running."

Treadgold hurried up the street.

As he neared The Buckskin, he saw Logan Thorn standing in the shade of the boardwalk across the street from the saloon. Logan wasn't trying to conceal himself. He leaned with casual insolence against an upright, his saddle gun racked on a shoulder, hat brim pulled low against the slant of the brittle, whiskey-colored morning sun. He touched

149

the hat brim with his free hand, acknowledging Treadgold's presence. The doctor couldn't see Logan's features, but he knew the eldest Thorn would be wearing a wolfish smile.

Reaching the saloon, Treadgold dodged a man bulling his way through the batwings, muttering oaths. The man was pulling off his canvas apron. He balled it up and hurled it to the ground, thoroughly disgusted.

"Good morning, Les," said Treadgold.

"Good for you, maybe," snapped the bartender. "Me, I just had a pistol waved in my face, so I've had better mornings."

"Bob Daggett and John Foley?"

"Yeah. And Rike Bartell's in there, too. The sorry cuss."

"Why did they pull iron on you?"

"Like a fool I told 'em we weren't open for business yet. They ain't in no mood to take no for an answer, and I ain't in no mood to get my ticket punched over a lousy bottle of nose paint."

Glancing over the barkeep's shoulder, Treadgold spotted Gantry and Zach Thorn coming up the middle of the street, walking side by side.

"I'd advise against going in there," said Les, accurately judging Treadgold's intentions. "They've got their hackles up and their hulls screwed down."

Treadgold nodded and then pushed through the batwings.

Rike Bartell and Bob Daggett, the latter with his arm in a sling, were belly up to the bar, slinging shots of liquid bravemaker. John Foley stood to the doctor's immediate left, watching Logan Thorn through the plate glass window. This early, there

150

was no one else in the saloon.

"Look at that, will you, Doc?" sneered Johnny. "That bastard Logan Thorn standing yonder like he owns Hell and half of Texas. I'm of a mind to shoot daylight through him."

The lanky redheaded youngster had an old Colt side-hammer rifle in a white-knuckled grip. A crazy light danced in his eyes.

"That's just what he wants you to try," said Treadgold, striving to keep his tone calm and measured.

"I'll do better'n try."

Treadgold walked to the bar, closer to Bob Daggett. If he was going to get any of them to see reason, he figured Bob would be the one.

"What are you doing, Bob?"

"Having a drink. What does it look like?"

"You shouldn't be here."

"Who says?"

"Ma Foley, for one."

"She don't run me."

"How about Watt? Does your father know you're here?"

Bob knocked back another strong dose of nerve medicine. When he brought the shotglass down on the mahogany, he did so with such force that the glass shattered in his hand. Rike Bartell jerked like a puppet on a string. He doused himself with whiskey. An unshaven, bleary-eyed man in old range clothes and down-at-heel boots, looking much older than his thirty-odd years, Rike stared, befuddled, at his wet shirt front.

"The lawman killed my brother," Bob growled, teeth clenched.

"And he's going to kill you," said Treadgold, quietly desperate, wanting to prevent bloodshed, knowing all along he would fail.

"We ain't scared," said Johnny.

"Hell no. We . . . we ain't scared," echoed Rike, with less conviction.

"Rike, you have no business being here," said Treadgold, pity in his voice. "You aren't even carrying."

A pistol lay on the bar—no doubt, thought Treadgold, the one Les the bartender had been threatened with. Now Bob slid the gun two feet to his left, so that it lay, turning slowly, in front of Rike.

"Now he's heeled," said Bob.

Rike watched the gun stop turning. It was pointed at his chest.

"Just walk away, Rike," urged Treadgold.

Bartell poured himself another shot. His hand was shaking. Amber whiskey sloshed onto the pistol and the bar.

"I ain't walkin'," said Rike. "Bob and Johnny, they're . . . they're my friends. 'Bout the onliest friends I got, and . . . and . . . well, I ain't walkin'."

"They're going to get you killed."

"So what?" muttered Rike. "You hear? So what? I don't care. Livin' ain't all it's cracked up to be."

Bob gave Rike a funny look. "Gantry's the one's gonna die."

Johnny took two steps back from the window, and by this alone Treadgold realized Gantry and Zach had joined Logan across the street, and that his time was up.

"Damn it," he said. He struck the bar with his fist. Daggett tensed into a crouch, sweeping back his duster, his hand falling to the gun in his belt. "Damn it!" Treadgold lost his temper. "Has everybody around here lost their minds? This stupid senseless feud! Go ahead, kill each other off. The world will be better for it. Pride. That's all it is. God Almighty. Stupid pride."

They just stared at him, taken aback by this outburst, so out of character. Treadgold regained his composure. He cleared his throat, tugged on his vest. He gave each of them in turn a look both scathing and pitying, then turned on his heel, and walked out of the saloon.

He crossed the street with long strides, stopped face to face with Zach Thorn.

"You're on the right side, Zach," he said calmly. "But for the wrong reasons."

He walked away, turning his back on all of them.

"Throw your guns out," called Gantry. "Then come out slow with your hands high."

"Make smoke!" screeched Bob Daggett.

Treadgold heard the crash of glass breaking, the deep-throated boom of side guns talking death.

He squeezed his eyes shut and walked on.

Chapter Twenty-Three

Bob Daggett fired the first shot. He pushed through the batwings, crossed the threshold, and began blazing away. A heartbeat later, Johnny Foley threw in, shooting through the plate glass window.

Gantry fired the Henry as fast as he could work the repeater's lever action. To his right, Logan had both Remingtons in action, triggering one and then the other, a deadly rhythm. The plate glass window disintegrated. Gun thunder rolled across the street. Gray smoke stung Gantry's eyes. He moved as he fired, a crouching sidestep. A bullet plucked at his longcoat, passed harmlessly through.

His charcoal-burner empty, Bob Daggett stepped back inside the saloon. The batwings creaked on their hinges as hot lead plowed through them. Bob broke open his Starr Army .44. Holding the revolver in his left hand, he plucked bullets out of his belt and reloaded.

Johnny was crawling across the floor, dragging himself away from the window through glass shards.

"I'm hit," gasped Johnny, white as a sheet. "I'm hit."

Bob's ears were ringing. The shooting had subsided. A temporary lull in the action, the eye of a hurricane. He felt remarkably calm, almost detached. He gazed impassively at Johnny, saw the dark crimson stain spreading on the youngest Foley's shirt front, just above the belt buckle.

Johnny was gutshot. Good as dead. Bob felt no regret, no pity for Foley. Instead, he was angry, feeling as though Johnny had let him down by getting himself so quickly killed.

He looked around for Bartell.

Rike was on his knees in front of the bar, one hand clutching the brass foot rail, the other arm raised, with the hand gripping the top edge of the mahogany. His head was bowed. He looked like a man deep in prayer. When the shooting started, his legs had gone rubbery. He had slumped to the ground, suddenly nauseated.

Walking over, Bob jammed the Starr's barrel against Rike's skull.

"You lily-livered bastard," said Bob coldly. "Get on your feet or I'll blow your head off."

Trembling, the seedy no-account pulled himself upright and leaned heavily against the bar for support. He groped for a bottle. Bob swept it out of his reach. It went spinning off the bar, shattered on the floor. Rike jumped.

"This ain't my fight!" he whined, terrified.

Bob's nose wrinkled. He took a backward step.

"Christ!" he said, disgusted, seeing the dark stain in the crotch of Rike's trousers. Bartell had soiled himself.

Outside, eyes narrowed against drifting gunsmoke, Gantry looked to his left. Zach Thorn was sprawled on his back in the dust of the street, a blue bullet hole an inch above his right eye. Blood pooled beneath his head. His eyes were wide open, filled with surprise.

Logan brushed past Gantry. Holstering his empty six-guns, he sat on his heels beside Zach's body. His head dipped down. He reached out, then closed his youngest brother's sightless eyes. As he rose, he scooped up the scattergun Zach had carried from the jail.

"Sorry, Logan," said Gantry.

Guilt wrenched at his insides. He felt responsible. Lying there dead in the dust, Zach looked like what he was: a boy. A half-grown youngster. Gantry told himself he'd had no business letting a boy buy into this.

Logan broke open the double-barreled shotgun.

"Didn't even get off a shot." He looked at Gantry, his eyes bright, a crooked smile fixed on his tightly pulled features, then swung his gaze across the street at the Buckskin Saloon. "I'll go in the back," he said, and started across. Blood squished in his boot. His pants leg was blood-soaked. But he didn't limp, didn't seem to notice he'd been hit.

Discarding the empty repeater, Gantry drew the Dragoon Colt from his holster. He hammered back, rolled the cylinder along his arm—in this way checking the old horse pistol's workings—then lowered the hammer. With a final bleak glance at Zach Thorn's body, he crossed the street. His stride was long and loose. He held the Colt down by his side, and watched the door and the shattered window. He didn't hurry, looking for all the world like a man on his way to a Sunday social rather than a killing.

As he reached the boardwalk, Bob Daggett appeared suddenly in the window.

"This is for Jesse, you sonuvabitch."

Bob swept his arm up. Gantry dived and fired at the same time. Daggett's Starr barked and spat flame. He rocked on his heels as Gantry's bullet struck him high in the shoulder, at a sharp upward angle. Gantry hit the warped and weathered planks and rolled, heard Bob's gun speak again, felt the sting of hot lead laying a furrow across his thigh.

On his back, Gantry extended his gun arm, and, as Daggett stepped out through the glassless window to line up his next shot, rolled the Colt's hammer back and squeezed the trigger. The hogleg jumped in his hand. Bob hunched forward, firing straight down into the boardwalk. He tottered, knock-kneed, like a man after one too many drinks of strong-water. He struggled to lift the Starr, as though the pistol weighed as much as an anvil.

Gantry fired again. This time he elected to go for a head shot. The bullet struck Bob's cheekbone, removed half the face in a mist of blood and bone fragments. Daggett fell in a spinning descent. The Starr clattered on the boardwalk. Bob's boot heels drummed the planking, his body twitching in death spasms.

Getting up, Gantry tested his leg, confirmed that it was only a graze, and dismissed the injury from his mind. His rib hurt him a lot worse—felt like an iron spike had been driven through his midsection.

He pushed resolutely through the bullet-riddled batwings. He didn't go in fast and low, like a participant in a gunfight, but rather more like a man casually strolling in to have a drink.

A redheaded youngster was curled in a fetal position on the floor, lying on his side with his arms locked tightly around his middle. The front of his clothes were slick with blood.

"Don't shoot!"

The shriek raked across Gantry's nerves. He flinched, brought the Dragoon Colt up fast. Then he saw Rike Bartell, and realized two things right off. One was that Rike posed no threat. Bartell was walking backwards, his hands held out in front of him. He bumped into a table, stumbled over a deal chair. Fear wrenched a strangled incoherent cry from him as the marshal's big horse pistol swung in his direction. He turned and broke for the back door.

Gantry understood then that the young man on the floor had to be John Foley. He dismissed Bartell as unworthy of further attention, and looked long and hard at the youngest Foley brother. Johnny wasn't much older than Zach Thorn. He wasn't dead yet, but he was more than halfway across the river.

Watching Foley die slow, Gantry felt a curious emptiness. He questioned many things in that half minute. Himself. His job. He didn't know if it was his bullet that killed Foley, or Logan's, and it really didn't matter. What mattered was that two young men—three, if you counted the somewhat older Bob Daggett—had lost their lives in a brief but fierce inferno of violence, and Gantry, for a moment, was sick of seeing young men die.

The deadly roar of a shotgun turned him away from Foley, and he saw Rike Bartell hurled backward from the Buckskin's rear door. Bartell's corpse landed on a table, with such force that the table broke into kindling.

Logan stepped through the doorway. He broke open the scattergun, turned it to spill the empty shells, and closed it with a sharp flick of the wrist. Ignoring Bartell entirely, he walked the length of the saloon and stood looking down at John Foley with strong satisfaction.

"Worth the cost?" asked Gantry. His tone was cold and cutting, like winter wind.

"What do you think?"

"I think you killed an unarmed man."

"Was he?" asked Logan, indifferent. "I didn't feel like taking a chance that he wasn't."

Gantry stepped outside. Treadgold was coming along the street, medical bag in hand. He went first to Zach. A glance told him the story there, and he hardly broke stride, veering across the street to peer at Bob Daggett's remains on the saloon boardwalk. He looked at Gantry, condemnation in his eyes, and Gantry had to force himself to meet the doctor's incriminating gaze.

"So this is law and order," said Treadgold.

Logan emerged from the saloon. As he passed Gantry, he handed the marshal the shotgun, and limped toward Zach's body.

"Logan!" Gantry's voice snapped like a whip.

Thorn stopped dead in his tracks. He didn't turn around.

"It was cold-blooded murder, Logan."

"He threw in with them. He paid the price. What are you going to do about it, Marshal? Arrest me?"

Gantry considered it. He wasn't forgetting that Logan had saved his life. Or that Logan had seen his brother die. Or even that in the chaotic fury of a life-and-death fight, one could not always afford to wait and see if the enemy was armed.

He owed Logan Thorn. But if he paid the favor back now, by letting Logan get away with murder, he was going to have to forfeit everything he stood for and believed in.

Logan smiled coldly. He misread Gantry's indecision as fear. He started walking again.

"I'm taking my brother home," he threw over his shoulder, the words strongly seasoned with disdain. "If you want to *try* arresting me, you'll know where I am."

He picked his brother up, carried him down the street in his arms, making for the horses hitched in front of the jail.

Gantry watched him go, vaguely aware of Treadgold entering the saloon behind him, aware also of the street—empty as a cowboy's pockets a moment before—beginning to fill with the curious.

He was still standing there a couple of minutes later, when Treadgold came back out onto the boardwalk.

"I'll take John and Bob out to Jestro's place in a wagon," said the doctor wearily. "Jestro will get them home."

Gantry nodded.

"Well, Marshal, looks like you lost your deputies. And just when you needed them most. Watt Daggett and the rest of the Foleys are going to come for your hide now."

"No," said Gantry. "I'll go to them."

Chapter Twenty-Four

Early the next morning, in a penitent mood, Doc Treadgold went again to the Tenaha jail.

An apron-faced sorrel stood hitched to the tie rail, ears down, head hanging, and one hind foot drawn up on the hoof tip. The three-quarter saddle on its back was cinched tight. Gantry's Henry rode in a saddle bucket. A blanket roll was tied on behind the cantle.

Treadgold paused on his way in to glance curiously at a shattered pane of glass in the front window.

Gantry was standing at the desk, putting a couple boxes of ammunition into his saddlebags.

"Looks like you're going to war," observed Treadgold.

"On the mark, Doc."

Treadgold noticed the strap-iron cells in back were empty. This was the first time they'd been unoccupied since Gantry's takeover of Tenaha almost a week ago. Some of the local men had been hardheaded, unwilling to check their weapons or abide by the curfew.

"I came to apologize, Marshal."

"What for?"

"My remarks yesterday. Had a lot of time to think it over. All the way out to Jestro's place. All the way back. All last night."

Gantry strapped the saddlebags closed.

"No need. You told it the way you saw it. My father gave me two rules to live by. Walk tall, talk straight. I reckon you talked plenty straight. I push too hard sometimes."

Treadgold noticed the marshal's haggard features. He realized he hadn't been the only one spending a sleepless night soul-searching.

"I was an army doctor. Fresh out of medical school when the war started. I served with Hood's Texans. So I saw plenty of killing, as Hood was usually in the middle of the fight. I think Sherman said it best. War is hell. Just three words. They say it all. I saw more suffering and death than any one person should have to see. I thought I'd get used to it after a while. But I never did. I put a higher value on human life when I came out of the war than I did when I went into it. That's why I said what I said."

"Fair enough."

"I think I had a problem with the war. I saw so many good men give up their lives, that I began to question the validity of the cause they fought for. Didn't seem like any cause could be worth so high a cost. But they were willing to die for what they thought was right, even if I didn't think it was. Maybe all of them were right, and I was wrong. I just wish sometimes people would solve their problems with common sense rather than cartridges."

"That would suit me down to the ground."

"But it will never happen, will it?"

Gantry draped the saddlebags over his shoulder. "I doubt it, sometimes."

"Because if all people were like that, we wouldn't have to have laws, or lawmen."

Gantry smiled. "You're a good man, Doc. Said it before. Too bad there aren't enough folks like you to go around."

He walked out. His spurs sang against the boardwalk. The street was empty; the town was just waking to the new day. Treadgold followed, stood in the cool shade, and watched Gantry tie the saddlebags to his rig.

"You're going after Luke Foley." It wasn't a question.

Gantry fished a crumpled piece of paper from a pocket of his longcoat, handed it to Treadgold as he freed rein leather from the tie rail. Treadgold read:

LUKE FOLEY AT MY PLACE. BRING RE-
WARD MONEY WITH YOU. BELLE

"Came through the window last night," said Gantry. "Wrapped around a rock. There's a map on the other side."

Treadgold said, "It's a trap."

"Reckon so."

"But you're going anyway."

"Without the reward money."

"It isn't money they're after."

"I know."

"Then why go? Luke's not at Belle Diamond's place. He can't be. I saw him a few days ago, laid up at the Foley cabin in Big Cypress Swamp, and he

163

wasn't going anywhere for a while."

"Maybe I'll get to make the acquaintance of the other Foley brothers."

Treadgold crushed the paper in his fist. "Won't be just Matt and Mark Foley. The odds will be too high for one man. Ma Foley said she was going to smoke you out. You're crazy if you go. You don't even think you'll make it back. That's why you emptied the jail, isn't it?"

Gantry climbed into the saddle. Treadgold stepped off the boardwalk, grabbed the cheekstrap of the sorrel's bridle to detain him.

"You get yourself killed and the Foleys win."

"They can't win. Another will come to take my place. Another after him, if need be."

"At least get the Thorns and the Tennallys to back you up."

"You told Zach he was on the right side for the wrong reason."

"At least he was on the right side."

"Not good enough," said Gantry, brusquely. "Makes the whole thing wrong. I should've seen that. And I should have seen the boy in Zach and the killer in Logan."

"I'm surprised you're not going after Logan."

"I'm the one to blame for Rike Bartell's death. I as much as gave Logan license to kill him."

"What about Joshua?"

"They say if you want a job done right, you do it yourself."

"Famous last words."

"I never knew my Uncle Ty, but I heard a lot about him when I was growing up," said Gantry. "He fought for Texas in the Revolution. Got himself captured by the Mexicans down around Refugio. He was sentenced to die by firing squad. They put him up against a wall and went to shooting. He took twenty slugs, and not one a killing shot. The *teniente* in charge of the firing squad was mighty put out, as you can imagine. He walked up to my uncle, drew his pistol, fired point-blank. The bullet just grazed Uncle Ty. Well, Uncle Ty was pretty sick and tired of the whole business by then. He said some uncomplimentary things about Mexican marksmanship. Said if they couldn't get the job done, he would. He asked the officer for the loan of his pistol, loaded it, and blew his own head off. At least, that's the story."

"Somehow," said Treadgold, horrified, "that sounds like a Gantry."

Gantry took a long look at the street. "Folks here have seen the Foleys ride roughshod over the rules and rights of others for a long spell. They wonder why they should have to walk the line themselves. Once the Foleys get their comeuppance, the rest will take care of itself."

"But you might not be around to see it."

Treadgold released the cheekstrap. Gantry neck-reined the horse, then checked it, turned in the saddle to look back at Treadgold.

"Look after Mercy, Doc. She's a nice girl. Deserves better than she's gotten so far."

"I think she'd rather you looked out for her yourself."

Gantry raised a hand in farewell, squared his shoulders, and rode out of Tenaha.

Chapter Twenty-Five

That same morning Zach Thorn was buried, a hundred paces from the cabin under the clump of pines where his parents and Logan's wife lay in their final rest. The Tennallys attended; Bull and Frank and Bull's wife and two children. Mercy noticed that all the men wore their Sunday-go-to-meeting suits, and every one carried a rifle and a side gun.

Business as usual in the Redlands, she mused. War and revenge. Killin' and buryin'. These men did not feel safe even in their own homes.

It was a beautiful spring morning. Cardinals in flight were flashes of scarlet among the evergreens. Robins and grackles flocked to the newly plowed fields. A cool breeze rustled the treetops, and the sun caressed the earth with a warm golden touch.

Yesterday the grave had been dug, the coffin built. All night Zach had lain in his pine box on a table in Logan's cabin. Mrs. Tennally had wept. So had Laura, sensitive to her husband's pain. Logan had gotten drunk. He remained quiet and unapproachable. Everyone gave him a wide berth, feeling the heat of the anger simmering inside him.

Only the children had slept. The men talked in fits and starts. They would tell stories about Zach. How he had done this on one occasion, and that on another. After each fond recollection, they would lapse into disconsolate silence.

Mercy was relieved that the night was finally over. Glad that Zach was being put in the ground. She felt a little ashamed of herself, but the whole ritual was very trying. Part of it was the fact that she was an outsider. The balance was sheer emotional exhaustion. She had a tremendous store of compassion. She hated to see others suffer, and felt their pain.

She realized the others were reluctant to consign Zach's mortal remains to that deep hole in the red clay. They did not want to part with him. There was something so very final about the burying. Mercy thought the burying wrenched as hard on the heart as the dying.

Joshua carried the family Bible. He read over Zach. Psalms 139.

"'If I should say "Surely the darkness will cover me," then the night would become light around me; for even darkness does not hide from Thee, but night is as bright as day. Darkness is the same as light to Thee. My bones are not hidden from Thee. In Thy book all was recorded and prepared day by day, when as yet none of them had being. How precious to me are Thy thoughts, O God. How vast is the sum of them. If I tried to count them, they would be more numerous than the sand. When I awake, I am still with Thee.'"

Last night Joshua had entered the date, next to Zach's name and his date of birth. The Thorn family

Bible contained two complete pages of birth and deaths, and part of a third. It had been brought across the sea, and then across the wilderness. Passed down from generation to generation. Mercy thought about all those people, wondered what they had been like, what their lives had been like. Now they were dust, and all that remained of them were entries in the Bible.

No, that wasn't all. There was blood. The blood flowing in the veins of the two Thorn brothers still living. The blood that had been spilled yesterday in the dust of a Tenaha street. And the ghosts of the people whose names filled two and a half pages in the Thorn family Bible cried out for more blood, because their own had been spilled.

Life had never seemed so fleeting, so cheap, and so precious as it did to Mercy that night.

Now Logan was taking the Bible from his brother. He leafed through the pages, scowling. Then, his eyes feverishly bright, he stabbed at a page with a finger, and read.

"'Do not go fretful on account of evildoers. Be not envious of the workers of wickedness. For like the grass they shall be quickly cut down.'"

He clapped the Bible shut, and glanced at Bull Tennally. Mercy saw Bull's almost imperceptible nod.

Logan surrendered the Bible to Joshua. He began shoveling dirt into the grave. It thumped onto the top of Zach's coffin. His movements were sharp, his expression turbulent. He seemed to be in a big hurry all of a sudden. Bull and Frank pitched in. When it was done, Logan leaned heavily on the shovel, drenched with sweat. Mercy thought he had a fever on account of the gunshot wound in his leg. He had insisted on doing his share of the grave digging, in spite of the wound.

For a moment no one moved, as though they were loath to leave Zach alone. It was Joshua who broke this dismal melancholy inertia. He put an arm around Laura and started back for the cabin, the Bible tucked under the other arm. The others straggled after him.

They were shy of the cabin when the sound of a horse at hard gallop reached them. Heads and gun barrels swung toward the sound.

"It's Doc Treadgold," said Joshua.

The doctor's horse was lathered stem to stern. It set back on hind legs as Treadgold sawed on the reins. He stayed in the saddle as the horse pranced and blew.

"Gantry's headed for Belle Diamond's," he announced. "It's a trap. The Foleys are going to ambush him."

Joshua looked at his brother. Logan had mentioned his falling out with Gantry, and Joshua was curious to know what Logan's reaction to this new development would be.

Logan, in turn, was gazing at Mercy.

"Let him fight his own fights," he said. "We'll fight ours."

"No," said Joshua, deeply disappointed. "Bull? Frank?"

The Tennally brothers were watching Logan. Joshua realized that imploring them to follow his lead, rather than Logan's, would be a futile exercise. They had always looked to Logan for leadership. Logan was the oldest, and he was so much like their father. Joshua, away for several years, had little influence over them.

"I thought you were a better man," Treadgold admonished Logan.

"You can keep your opinions to yourself," said Logan darkly.

"I'm going," said Joshua.

"You ain't," snapped Logan.

"Don't try to stop me, Logan. I may, as you said, talk fancified, but I'm still a Thorn."

Joshua turned toward the cabin. Laura clutched at his arm, dragging on him like an anchor.

"Don't go, Joshua. If you love me, don't go."

"It's because I love you that I *am* going."

Reaching the cabin porch, he disentangled himself. Laura sank to the steps, a stunned expression on her face. Mercy went to her.

"You got to let a man do man things," said Mercy. "He's got to do them, or he don't feel like he's a whole man. And if he don't feel that way, he can't make you feel like a whole woman."

Laura stared at her blankly, as though she was talking gibberish. Mercy assumed she wasn't getting across.

Then Laura said, "But he doesn't know. If he knew, he wouldn't go."

"Know what?"

"He's going to be a father."

Mercy looked around. No one was close enough to hear.

"You sure?"

"Of course."

Of course, thought Mercy. A stupid question. A woman knew such things. Her body told her.

"Why haven't you told him?"

"I don't know. I wasn't certain of it until several days ago. And then . . . all of this . . ." Laura made a helpless gesture. "Should I tell him now, Mercy? If I do, I will keep him from doing what he thinks is right. Will he hate me for that?"

"He'll never hate you," said Mercy. "But I can't tell you what to do. You have to decide yourself."

Thinking about the Thorn family Bible, and about a new entry that would soon be made in it, Mercy left her there on the porch steps and slipped around behind the cabin.

Treadgold climbed down off his horse to stretch the stiffness out of his back and legs. He watched Logan and the Tennally boys palaver, but heard none of their soft-spoken words. A moment later the Tennallys got into a spring wagon, the children in the back, and pulled away. Logan entered the cabin. Treadgold expected to hear the sounds of a knock-down-drag-out between the two Thorn brothers. He glanced at Laura, felt sorry for her; wanted to provide words of comfort. But for once, words failed him.

A few minutes later Joshua emerged from the house, dressed in rougher clothes now, carrying a Winchester rifle and a rolled blanket. He did not even look at Laura, studiously avoided looking at her, and she did not look up at him. He leaned the rifle against a porch post, dropped the blanket roll in a rocking chair, and started around the cabin. Joshua pulled up short as Mercy led two saddled horses around the corner.

"What are you doing?" Joshua asked her.

"I'm goin' with you."

"No, you're not."

171

"Yes, I am."

Joshua turned to Treadgold for support. The doctor studied Mercy for a moment. Just a wisp of a girl, hardly big enough to throw shadow. She just stood there in a calico dress, barefoot, yellow hair in her eyes. Gantry had asked him to look out for her, and he felt he ought to talk her out of going, but he saw failure down that road. Besides, he no more wanted to tangle with Mercy than he did a bobcat.

"There'll be no stopping her," he warned Joshua. "She'll go, with or without us."

"Us? You riding with me, Doc?"

Treadgold nodded.

"Might be some killing," said Joshua.

"I'll do everything in my power to prevent it."

Joshua shook his head, took the reins of his horse from Mercy. She swung aboard a gray gelding. Treadgold recognized it as the horse on which she had come into Tenaha, riding with Gantry and his erstwhile prisoners, Watt and Bob Daggett. She forked the saddle like a man.

Logan stepped out of the cabin, watched Mercy, a sullen and dangerous look on his face.

"You're staying with me," he said.

"I ain't," she replied, defiantly.

Treadgold could read Logan's inner turmoil on the man's features. Logan was taken with Mercy, that was plain enough. But if he had ever known how to be gentle, how to ask rather than demand, Logan had long ago forgotten. He knew how Mercy felt about Gantry, and it galled him, clouded his thinking. For this reason, more than any other, he was willing to let Gantry ride into bushwhack.

"Get down off that horse, girl," ordered Logan.

"You think just 'cause you give me this dress you own me?" she asked hotly. "Well, you can have your durned ol' dress if you want, but you can't never have me, Logan Thorn."

Treadgold thought for a moment that Mercy was going to shuck the dress right then and there, in front of God and everybody. But Logan backed down, and she didn't have to go so far to prove her point. He spun on his heel and retreated into the cabin.

Rising from the porch steps, Laura gathered up her husband's bed roll and long gun and took them to him. Surprised, Joshua stepped into the saddle, took the rifle from her and booted it, draped the blanket roll across the saddle in front of him. She put a hand on his thigh.

"Come back to me, Joshua. I'll be waiting. You do what you have to do. Put a stop to this, once and for all. So that your children won't have to live in fear. I'll be here waiting for you."

He bent down and kissed her.

"Nothing and nobody could keep me from coming back to you, Laura," he declared.

She smiled bravely and stepped away.

Treadgold mounted up. He knew exactly what Laura was thinking at that moment.

There was one thing that *could* keep Joshua from coming back to her.

A bullet.

Chapter Twenty-Six

Gantry figured it was a cinch that Treadgold was right—the message from Belle Diamond was meant to lure him into ambush.

The road brought him out of the piney woods and across a wooden bridge, spanning a sluggish brown bayou. Beyond a weed-overgrown levee stood fields of sugarcane, long neglected, growing more than twenty feet high and arching over the road ahead. At the end of the road, maybe a quarter-mile distant, stood an old plantation house. He couldn't see all of it, and only the uppermost branches of the big black oaks and pecans, draped with Spanish moss, that stood about it.

Dismounting, he climbed to the rim of the levee and got a better look, sitting on his heels in the tall weeds. He spotted no activity around the house. It was quiet. Too quiet. Most likely, they were waiting for him in the house, their horses hidden, their guns ready. Had they seen him, coming out of the woods and crossing the bridge? He didn't know and didn't particularly care.

The wind moved through the cane. The stalks clacked and clattered like a thousand telegraph keys. They wouldn't be lurking in the cane. It was virtually impenetrable.

Gantry wondered idly what had befallen the original owners. A lot of hard work had been invested in this place. Pushing back the forest, building the levee, digging the irrigation ditches, harvesting what looked to be about a square mile of sugarcane. It must once have been a thriving plantation. Molasses, rum, and alcohol were money-making byproducts of this crop.

Years ago, the house had been a handsome home. The first floor was constructed of red clay bricks, to provide a sturdy foundation and withstand the occasional flood. A front staircase led to the upper floor by way of a wide gallery. Ivy covered the four tapered columns extending across the front of the house. The cypress clapboard of the second-story exterior walls, once painted a pristine white, were molded and peeling. Some window shutters were missing, others hung lopsided, hinges broken. The roof of cypress shingles was in an extreme state of disrepair. Around the house stood a few out-buildings: kitchen, smokehouse, four-holer. Way off across the fields stood a row of derelict shanties—the slave quarters.

Gantry rolled a smoke, considering his options. Some good could be said for putting your head down and barging straight ahead into trouble. He'd seen his father use the walk-'em-down technique to good effect, and he'd used it himself on many occasions. You could rattle a lot of men with that bold-as-brass approach—men who weren't as hardcase as they thought themselves to be. You could wade into a whole passel of walleyed, trigger-happy bravos, and sometimes they would back down, because they would wonder if maybe you had an edge they didn't know about, some good reason for not being afraid of the odds.

But Gantry didn't think that the men he was up against this time were the type to back down. He'd met two of the Foley brothers already. He could vouch for their courage, though he could find little else good to say about them. The Foleys did not back down, and it followed that the men who rode with them would not either. Brave men did not brook cowards in their company.

Treadgold's warning came back to him. *Ma Foley said she was going to smoke you out.*

Pale blue eyes ranging across the canefields, Gantry smiled.

What worked for Ma Foley would work for him, sure as Hell was hot.

He descended the embankment, crossed an empty irrigation ditch, and, at the edge of the canefield west of the road, began pulling up clumps of grass and weeds, piling it against the cane. He worked his way along the ditch about a hundred yards, leaving a heap of fire fodder every ten yards or so. Building another cigarette, he took a few drags off the quirly and then retraced his steps, dipping the cigarette into each pile, moving on when the dry weeds began to curl in a ripple of smoke.

Reaching the road, he retrieved the sorrel and led it down into the ditch that paralleled the levee, walking away from the road, heading east. A few minutes later, he could hear the fire catching hold of the cane and looked over his shoulder. Black waves of smoke rolled across the field west of the road, moving in the direction of the house. Tongues of flame consumed the writhing stalks of sugarcane, driven by the southerly breeze.

Gantry pressed on, and in time arrived at another road, cutting through the cane between house and levee. Down this he turned, heading for the house. The fire was roaring, and great black drifts of smoke filled the sky.

Nearing the point where the road emerged from the canefields, he mounted up and put the reins in his teeth. The Henry repeater came out of the saddle boot, and the Dragoon Colt out of its holster. He spurred the sorrel into a lope.

Coming out of the canefields, he rode toward the east side of the house. A pall of acrid smoke hung beneath the shade trees. The cane to the south of him was a raging inferno. Fire had leapfrogged the road into the adjacent field. It made its own wind, and the trees danced like dervishes. Gantry realized the house might also burn. He had intended a diversion, not total destruction. The best laid plans . . .

A woman came running out the back of the house. She wore pantalets and a camisole. She didn't see him. But someone inside the house did. Window glass shattered. A gun spoke. He saw the blossom of orange flame from a gun barrel. The man's aim was off. Gantry fired revolver and rifle simultaneously. He guided the horse with his knees, angling for the northeast corner of the plantation house. Another spurt of flame from the window; again Gantry blazed away. Smoke burned his eyes and made them water. Dimly, he saw a man rise up in the window, then pitch forward, crashing through to hang, arms dangling, over the sill.

Spitting out rein leather, Gantry executed a running dismount. He reached the back staircase of the house and collided with another woman coming down in a big hurry. She wore a long chemise and nothing else. He glimpsed a heavily painted face twisted with fear, carrot-colored hair in wild disarray. She cursed him with the flair of a sailor, and in trying to push past him lost her balance and tumbled down the steps, pale arms and legs all akimbo.

When he gained the back porch, the lawman could see through open double doors down a wide hallway running the length of the second story, north-south. As he passed through the doorway, a man stepped into the hall from one of the rooms. A big man, with a bandolier carrying shotgun shells across his bare chest.

It was Jestro. Seeing Gantry, he whirled, scattergun at hip level. Gantry dived forward as the shotgun roared. Double-ought buck splattered the door frame. Sliding on the pine floor, Gantry fired the Dragoon Colt. Jestro shuddered, dropped to his knees.

Gantry got to his feet. Jestro, hunched over, was breaking open the shotgun. He plucked the spent shells from the weapon, coughed, seemed to have some trouble getting new loads out of the bandolier loops. Gantry walked closer, thumbing back the Dragoon's hammer.

"Don't do it," he said.

178

Jestro looked up at him, coughed again. This time blood spilled over his lower lip and into his beard. He fumbled with the shells, trying to reload the shotgun, as though he were blind and trying to accomplish the task by feel.

"Give it up," said Gantry.

Jestro finally got a shell into place. He snapped the scattergun shut. Gantry fired the Dragoon Colt, point-blank range.

"Marshal!"

Gantry turned. A man stepped out of one of the rooms off the hallway. His hair was rust red, his eyes gunmetal gray. This one had to be a Foley, thought Gantry. He looked too much like Luke not to be.

He held a woman in front of him, an arm hooked tightly around her throat, a pistol to her head. She was thin, hollow-cheeked, pretty—a mulatto. She wore a frayed silk wrapper and an expression of dull despair.

"Drop your guns, lawman, or I'll kill her."

Gantry's blood ran cold.

Just like Kid Spence. With a gun to his mother's head.

Twenty years and then some had passed, but the image was branded into his mind. As vivid as though it had happened yesterday.

And now he was standing in his father's place, and the same terrible decision was his to make.

"Don't believe me?" snarled Foley. He pressed the gun harder against the woman's head. "Tell him, sister."

"Matt, please . . ."

He pushed harder still. *"Tell him, bitch!"*

179

"He'll do it, mister," she said, the hopeless whisper of one resigned to her fate.

Gantry stared at her. She didn't in the slightest look like his mother. Yet he saw his mother standing there. Plain as day.

Though he did not know her, this woman's survival suddenly meant everything to him. Her plight rendered him helpless, because at that moment, with perfect clarity, he understood fully and for the first time what wearing the badge signified.

She was an innocent, caught in the middle, swept up in a whirlwind of violence, as his mother had been, and it was his job to protect her.

He saw his mother in her, yet he didn't see Kid Spence in Matt Foley, and he knew why. He'd indicated to Joshua Thorn that he wore a star because it gave him the right to hunt down men like Kid Spence. But that just wasn't a good enough reason. To put his life on the line—just as he had seen his father do, time and time again—to protect the innocents caught in the middle, was a far better one.

Gantry dropped his guns.

"Mark, where the hell are you?" Matt yelled. To Gantry he said, "Kick those irons away."

Gantry complied. The Henry and the Colt skittered across the pine flooring. Mark clambered up the stairs from the first floor. He took it all in with a glance. Then he plowed into Gantry, driving him into a wall, sticking the barrel of his side gun into Gantry's slab-hard midsection.

"You killed my little brother, you sonuvabitch!"

Matt pushed the woman away, stepped in to intercede.

"Ma wants him alive, Mark."

"I want him dead."

"Oh, he'll die," promised Matt, glancing at Gantry, looking for fear in the marshal's cold blue eyes, and finding not a trace.

"He killed Johnny."

"Johnny went into Tenaha against Ma's orders. It's his own fault he's gone under."

A growl welling up in his throat, Mark slammed the pistol against the side of Gantry's head. Gantry sagged, fought to keep his legs under him, but made not a sound. Mark struck again and again in savage fury. The fourth blow did the trick. Gantry pitched forward, saw the floor rushing up through a scarlet swimming haze, but he didn't feel the floor. Just kept falling, falling . . .

Chapter Twenty-Seven

Joshua, Treadgold, and Mercy smelled the smoke long before they reached Belle Diamond's place, so the sight that greeted them as they rode out of the woods and crossed the bayou-spanning bridge did not come as a total shock.

The canefields had been reduced to charred smoking stubble. Off to the west, the fire still raged, having reached the forest. Tall pines were columns of flame. The plantation house at the end of the road appeared to be untouched.

"What happened here?" muttered Joshua.

"Gantry happened," said Treadgold.

Mercy kicked the gray gelding into a high lope, surging ahead of the two men.

"Mercy!" yelled Joshua. "Be careful!"

Treadgold shook his head. "Shakespeare said love is blind. It's also deaf, apparently."

"Well, looks like it's all over anyway."

"Not 'til the fat lady sings," said Treadgold, urging his horse into a quicker gait.

As they neared the plantation house, Joshua spotted a woman sitting at the top of the front staircase. He recognized her as Belle Diamond. She was smoking a claro cigar. Clad only in pantalets and chemise, she leaned back on her elbows, legs carelessly spread in a very unladylike fashion. But then, mused Joshua, no one had ever mistaken Belle for a lady.

Behind Belle, on the gallery, were two bodies covered with sheets. Mercy jumped off her horse and bounded up the steps with the quick agility of a deer. Belle watched ambivalently as Mercy threw back the sheets to identify the dead.

"Jestro and Reuben Stalls," said Belle. "The lawman did for 'em."

"Where is he?" asked Mercy.

"Who do you mean? Watt Daggett?"

"The lawman."

Belle's hand fluttered, a gesture of immense indifference.

"They took him." A thought sparked her curiosity. "You taken up with the lawman, now, is that it, honey? I thought you belonged to Watt."

"I never belonged to him," said Mercy vehemently.

Joshua dismounted at the front of the staircase. There was a trace of irony in the way he touched his hat to Belle.

"Hello, Belle. How's business?"

Belle smirked. "As I live and breathe. Joshua Thorn. Heard you was back. What a pity."

Joshua climbed the stairs. "Anybody inside?"

"A few of the girls. The Foley bunch is gone."

"I'll take a look for myself, if you don't mind."

"Help yourself."

"You come with me, Belle."

Putting weight on her elbows, Belle raised her bony behind off the step and rolled her hips, a lascivious bump and grind.

"Want a poke, you gotta pay, cowboy."

"I'll pass."

Joshua's cool derision infuriated Belle. She jumped to her feet.

"Think you're too good, huh? Well, you ain't half the man Mark Foley is."

Joshua remained unruffled. Hers was not what could be called an objective point of view. It was a well-known fact Belle Diamond was partial to the Foleys, Mark in particular.

"Come on, Belle, Let's take a look inside."

"They're gone, I tell you. If they was in there, they'd shoot right through me anyhow, so you won't do any good hiding behind me. You're too late. They took the lawman."

"Took him where?"

"Big Cypress Swamp. Ma Foley wanted him brought to her alive."

"Was Watt here?" asked Mercy.

"Yeah. He wanted to curl that lawman's toes right off. So did Mark. But Matt said no. Wasn't the way Ma Foley wanted it done."

Joshua wondered what Ma Foley had in store for Gantry. Whatever it was, it wouldn't be pleasant.

"Who else besides the Foleys and Watt and these two?" he asked Belle, indicating the two laid out on the gallery.

"Three others. They was hopin' you and your

184

brother would be ridin' with the lawman."

"We should have been."

"Well, he was a handful all by his lonesome," Belle allowed. "Damn near burned me out. Wind shifted just in time. I must be livin' right, huh? But it spooked my girls. They ran like rabbits. A few come back already. Listen, if you happen upon some half-naked harlots wanderin' around in the woods, you tell 'em to get their lazy butts back here. We're still open for business. A little bloodletting ain't gonna close me down."

"You're a real trooper, Belle," said Joshua dryly.

"You should know, Joshua," she replied, with a salacious grin. "You've seen me ride."

Joshua shook his head, glanced at Treadgold. The doctor was sitting his horse at the foot of the staircase.

"I'd better take a look inside, Doc, just in case."

Treadgold nodded. Joshua entered the plantation house with all due caution, the Forehand & Wadsworth .38 drawn and hammered back. Belle watched him go with mild scorn, hands on hips, cigar jutting from her sardonic lips. Then she turned her attention to Treadgold.

"Got any of that mercury and arsenic, Doc?" She leered at Mercy. "I got a social disease."

"How about just arsenic, straight up," said Treadgold.

Belle feigned shock. "Now what did you go and say a thing like that for, Doc?"

"Why'd you do it, Belle? Why'd you write that note to Marshal Gantry?"

"Only reason I do anything. Money."

"Hey," said Mercy.

Belle turned. Mercy swung with all her might. Her fist caught Belle on the point of the chin. The cigar, bitten in two, fell out of Belle's mouth. Her eyes rolled up in their sockets. She tumbled down the staircase, limp as an empty glove.

Treadgold calmed his prancing horse, then dismounted to kneel beside Belle Diamond. She was out cold, nothing worse. He looked up at Mercy, standing at the top of the staircase, hands still balled into fists, a breath of wind tousling the yellow hair hanging unfettered over her eyes, and whipping the blue calico dress against her legs.

Running out of the house, Joshua took stock of the situation, peered in wonder at Mercy.

"You do that?"

She nodded, tight-lipped.

"Good girl."

He proceeded down the stairs to Treadgold.

"She hurt bad?" he asked.

"You could argue not bad enough."

"Why, Doc, if I didn't know better, I'd say you were taking sides. What about the Hippocratic Oath?"

"I'll worry abut my professional ethics later. Right now I want to know what we are going to do about Gantry."

"The odds are pretty steep," admitted Joshua.

"I know how we can even them up," said Mercy.

Both men turned to watch her coming down the stairs. She walked right past them and swung aboard the gray gelding, fierce determination stamped on her elfin features.

"Well?" she asked, impatient. "You men do a lot of talking about right and wrong. Now's your chance to

186

do something besides flap lip."

Joshua Thorn thought it over. A physician opposed to violence, a barefoot girl who could take a sit-down bath in a wagon track, and unquestionably the worst shot in the Thorn family . . . pitted against the deadliest owlhoots in the Texas Redlands.

"She doesn't beat around the bush," he told Treadgold.

"No, not much."

Joshua offered the .38 revolver. Treadgold was hesitant in accepting it.

"I don't know about this," he admitted.

"It's better to have it and not need it, than to need it and not have it. And I have a hunch you're going to need it before we're done."

Treadgold grimaced, put the gun in his medical bag, and headed for his horse.

Chapter Twenty-Eight

When Gantry came to, he was riding belly down across the saddle. Excruciating pain from his cracked rib cut him in half. He had difficulty breathing. But there was no help for it. He was lashed down with rope. His hands were tied behind his back. A rope was wrapped around his knees, carried under the barrel of his horse, looped about his chest, and then tied off to the saddle horn. His struggles were fruitless. Worse, they brought him to the attention of Watt Daggett.

Watt brought his horse alongside the sorrel. Grabbing a handful of Gantry's black hair, he wrenched the marshal's head up. He grinned when he saw the agony etched deeply into Gantry's face.

"Dead man's ride, remember, you bastard? Men been known to die, they ride too long like this."

Gantry had a rude response in mind, but he could scarcely breathe, much less carry on a conversation. All he managed was a kind of wheezing, pain-wracked grunt.

Watt chortled. "You shoulda killed me when you had the chance."

Gantry had to agree.

"You done for both my boys," continued Watt. "You stole my woman away from me. I'm gonna skin you alive."

He viciously drove Gantry's head down against the saddle fender. Compared to the white hot agony in his chest, Gantry hardly noticed the impact.

Watt's mention of Mercy brought a new kind of anguish. Gantry remembered how pretty she had looked in the dress Logan had given her. The way she'd held onto his arm that night in the Daggett cabin. Held on for dear life. She had reached out to him. He regretted not having reciprocated. Not for his sake, but for hers. She had shown him kindness and caring, and he had given nothing of himself in return. She deserved more than a cold shoulder. But he'd been afraid to give more. Now it looked to be too late.

He swam in and out of consciousness. The sorrel splashed through black water, sometimes fetlock-deep, sometimes as high as the hock. Dun-colored muck swirled up beneath the hooves. He came to, once, with his head and shoulders underwater. Alarmed, he gasped, a reflex that sucked water into his lungs. Writhing helplessly against his bindings, he thought for a moment that he was going to drown. The idea of dying so ignominiously infuriated him. Then the horse waded into more shallow water, and Gantry tried to breathe while he coughed and choked and puked the swamp out of his lungs. He heard a man's rough laughter, then surrendered himself to blessed oblivion.

Next time he came to he was hitting the ground. Hitting it hard. He lay there a moment, too stunned to move. His hands were still tied. Patches of blue sky were visible through interlaced branches of cypress trees draped with gray moss. The world tilted. His stomach performed a slow wretched roll. He turned on his side. Someone bestowed upon him a brutal kick to the groin, and he blacked out.

Cold, sour-smelling water dashed in his face brought him back. Now he was propped up in a sitting position against a log. Matt Foley was hunkered down in front of him. A gray gloom had gathered under the trees as night came creeping through the swamp. A fire crackled twenty paces behind Matt. Gantry wished he were closer to it; the evening's damp chill crept into his aching joints. His longcoat was gone. So were his boots. His bare feet were blocks of ice; the hard-twist around his ankles cut off all circulation.

"My brother fancied your boots," explained Matt. "Watt's got your coat. Me, I've had my eye on this."

He ripped the badge off Gantry's shirt.

"A little something to remember you by," grinned Matt. "You ain't gonna be needin' it."

He watched Gantry, expecting some kind of response. Gantry's face betrayed no emotion.

"You're a hard man," begrudged Matt. "Hard men die hard. We're gonna find out just how hard tomorrow."

He joined the others around the fire.

Gantry took a long look around. Swamp in all directions. The camp stood on a hummock, beneath cypress and tupelo trees, festooned with big clumps of saw grass. The air was alive with the chirrups and whistles of marsh creatures. When night fell, he saw countless pairs of white pinpricks in the deep darkness, the eyes of bullfrogs reflecting the firelight. And, too, the feral red gaze of the occasional gator.

No chance of escape—he accepted that. At least not now. The Foleys, Watt, and the three desperadoes he did not know by name had their supper, passed around a bottle of popskull, then rolled into their soogans. Watt Daggett took the first stretch of guard duty. He kept the fire fed and a malevolent eye on Gantry.

Tomorrow, then, they aimed to kill him. Gantry didn't give in to panic, and he didn't give up hope. Nothing he could do but wait for his chance. It might come, and then again it might not. Time would tell. What little time he had remaining to him.

He laid his head back on the soggy, worm-eaten log, and closed his eyes. Closed his mind to apprehensions about what tomorrow might bring, and to the bitter cold of the night, and the jarring pain every breath cost him. He went to sleep, and met Mercy in his dreams.

Next morning, they permitted him to ride upright in the saddle. A definite improvement. His hands remained tied behind his back—he could only assume he still had hands—he'd long since lost any sensation in them. Matt Foley led his horse by its reins. The others kept an eye on him. One wrong move and they would fill him full of lead. Watt, for one, was just waiting for the chance. His hellfire eyes bored into Gantry's back. Gantry assumed the only reason he was still among the living was because Ma Foley had something special planned in the way of his demise. Or maybe she just wanted the privilege of putting a bullet between his eyes for herself. Gantry tried not to think about what waited uptrail. He just watched for his chance.

It hadn't come by the time they reached the Foley place, a few hours later, a filthy ramshackle cabin on a spit of dry land, surrounded by rank dismal swamp. A pair of the ugliest, most vicious-looking hounds Gantry had ever seen howled at the ends of stout rope in paroxysms of raving fury, slaver spraying from snapping fangs.

"Shaddup, you goddam skillet-lickers!"

Ma Foley emerged from the cabin, supporting herself on a crutch. The dogs responded immediately to her screeching command, settling down on quivering haunches. Wheezing with exertion, Ma Foley stopped at the edge of the porch, the weathered planking creaking under her weight. She cocked her head to one side and squinted curiously at Gantry through her one good yellow eye.

"This him?" she asked.

Matt and the others had dismounted. Watt said, "Yeah, this is the sonuvabitch. Now you've seen him, let's end it."

"Don't be in such a hurry. Get him down."

Mark grabbed Gantry's left stirrup and lifted sharply. Gantry pitched sideways off the sorrel. With his hands tied, he could not break his fall. He landed on his side and fetched his head a ringing lick on the ground. Lancing pain pushed him to the brink of unconsciousness. He stubbornly resisted going over the edge. Rough hands jerked him to his feet, jostled him forward, closer to Ma Foley.

"You've caused me and mine a heap of grief, lawman," she said.

"Glad to hear it."

She snorted. "A man from the ground up, just like I figured. Know who I am?"

"I know."

"You're gonna rue the day you ever stepped foot into my country, Marshal."

"You've got more tallow on you than a herd of cattle," he sneered.

She grinned, showing crooked yellow teeth in blackened gums.

"Know what they say about fat women—warm in the winter, shade in the summer."

"Where I come from, they say a hog gets this big, kill it."

Mark Foley punched him in the face. Gantry cakewalked, trying to keep his feet, and failed. he landed within range of one of the hounds. The dog lunged. Gantry rolled desperately, and jaws clamped down on his left leg just above the knee. This time he couldn't keep from crying out, a guttural scream every bit as savage and primeval as the snarl of the beast gnawing his flesh into bloody pulp. Gantry kicked with his other leg, but couldn't dislodge the hound.

Ma Foley shrieked. The dog released Gantry, backed off, drooling blood and slobber. Gantry tried to sit up. The world began to spin madly. He gave it up, lay down, and squeezed his eyes shut.

"Somebody slap a tourniquet on that leg," said Ma.

"Hell," groused Watt. "Why bother? Let him bleed to death."

"Don't backtalk me, Watt. Do what I tell you or I'll have your balls for breakfast. Then bring him inside. Every man deserves one last shot of hunnerd-proof nerve medicine 'fore he meets his Maker."

Chapter Twenty-Nine

They picked him up and half-dragged him into the cabin. At Ma's direction, he was seated at the trestle table. She ordered his hands untied. A truculent Watt balked at that, but Mark pulled his knife and sliced the rope. Gantry grimaced at exquisite agony, a million needles pricking his skin as the blood rushed back into his hands.

Gusting a sigh of relief, Ma Foley settled her obese body into the wagon seat braced against the wall. Matt, Mark, and Watt Daggett stood around, restless. The other three outlaws waited outside on the porch. Everybody except Ma appeared anxious for the fun to start. She seemed to derive pleasure from the situation. Gantry was in no big hurry. He was still looking for his chance. Being untied was a step in the right direction, but it wasn't quite enough. Watt and the Foley boys watched him like hungry wolves, praying he'd make a move.

Ma took a swig from a jug of corn liquor. Smacking her lips, she wiped her chin with the back of her hand and held the jug out to Matt. The eldest Foley boy balanced the jug in the crook of his arm and had a long drink, gulping the strong-water down.

"Give our guest a drink, boy," said Ma. "Where's your manners?"

Matt put the jug on the table. Gantry knew how to handle a jug, too, and his drink was as long and deep as Matt's. Ma chuckled approvingly.

"How 'bout a cheroot, Marshal?"

The condemned man's last smoke, mused Gantry. Why was Ma playing this cat-and-mouse game? Trying to unnerve him, maybe. Wanting to see how much sand he really had.

"No thanks," he said. "But I wouldn't mind my own—except one of your kin took my makings."

"They are a tad light-fingered," owned Ma. "Runs in the family. Who's got this man's tobacky?"

"Christ!" muttered Watt. "Next thing you know, we'll be askin' him to sit down to vittles with us."

Mark Foley tossed Gantry's wheatstraw papers and muslin pouch of Lone Jack on the table. Gantry built a roll-your-own. He was pleased to see that his hands were quite steady. Ma Foley was also delighted.

"You bit off more'n you could chew this time, lawman," she said. "Shoulda kept out of the Redlands. Now you're gonna be stayin', permanent-like."

"Somebody got a match?" asked Gantry.

Matt scraped a lucifer on the table top, fired the tip of Gantry's cigarette.

"Done some damage, I'll give you that," continued Ma. "Watt's boys are dead, and my youngest. And I'm right concerned about Luke."

196

"Where is Luke, by the way?" asked Gantry. "I aim to take him on to Jefferson. They've got a rope up there with his name on it."

"Luke's in yonder." Ma nodded at a blanket-draped doorway. "Got a bad fever. Leg's all swole up. Gangrene, I reckon. Might lose it. You owe for that, on top of everything else." She peered at Matt. "I reckon the Thorns owe us, too."

Matt said, "Gantry came alone. Killed Jestro and Reuben."

"Alone?" Ma Foley lit a cheroot, puffed vigorously. "You go on your own hook, don't you, Marshal?"

"Didn't need any help," answered Gantry, figuring a little impudent bravado couldn't hurt him. "This nest of snakes is no hill for a stepper."

Watt snorted. "Bold talk from a man fixin' to cross the river."

"Well, we'll collect from the Thorns later," said Ma.

Gantry calmly loosened the tourniquet on his leg. Big dollops of blood splattered on the floor. He took another swig from the jug, a long drag on his cigarette, then tightened up the tourniquet. He felt light-headed and nauseous, but he didn't let it show. It was a rather ostentatious display of cool audacity, performed for Ma Foley's benefit. Personal bravery, even in an adversary, was a virtue she seemed to hold in high regard. It was evident to Gantry that if he betrayed even a trace of fear, these people would waste no more time with him, would shoot him down like a dog.

It was a game he had played before. One he understood and knew how to exploit. Where he came

197

from, Comanche warriors and Mexican *bandoleros* alike appreciated courage. In Gantry's opinion, the wisest course was to kill a brave man quick as you could. You could admire him later.

He recalled a story told about Stonewall Jackson. During the Battle of Second Manassas, one of Jackson's aides had expressed remorse upon witnessing the death of a Union officer, courageously leading his unit in a futile assault on Stonewall's lines. Jackson had gravely replied, "No, Captain. Kill the brave ones. They lead the others."

"So what are we gonna do?" Watt asked Ma. "Sit around here and play chin music all day long? I got better things to do."

Ma sighed and looked askance at Daggett. She reached over and picked up a gun lying on the wagonseat/chair. Her hand, Gantry noticed, was an arthritic claw, but she seemed very adept at handling a revolver, in spite of this deformity.

Gantry's life work had made of him an expert on firearms. He recognized Ma's weapon as a grapeshot pistol. Invented by Doctor Colonel Jean LeMat of New Orleans, it carried nine .44 caliber pinfire cartridges in its cylinder. Below the pistol barrel was a .60 caliber shotgun barrel. The single shotgun load could be fired by adjusting the hammer nose. An odd-looking but exceedingly deadly piece of artillery. Gantry had seen but a few in his time. Pinfire cartridges were difficult to obtain, and loading the gun was a pain in the neck.

"No," replied Ma. "We'll have our vengeance. But we're gonna give the Marshal here a fair chance."

"Fair chance?" yelped Watt in disbelief. "You must be kidding."

Ma ignored Daggett, turned to Gantry.

"You can go."

Gantry didn't move. His mind was racing. What was her game?

"Matt, you still got that timepiece?"

"Yeah, Ma."

Matt fetched a stemwinder out of his pocket, thumbed open the cover. Gantry wondered where he'd stolen it.

"You've got five minutes, lawman," announced Ma. "When the time's up, these fellers are gonna be comin' after you."

"This is crazy," complained Watt. "We coulda done for him at Belle's place. We dragged him halfway across the Big Cypress, just so's you could give him a 'fair chance'? Hell, he killed one of your sons, and both of mine."

Ma nodded. "He did that. And he did it fair and square. They had a chance, and he'll get the same. Your five minutes is runnin', Marshal."

Gantry glanced at the watch in Matt's hand, at the door, then back to Ma.

"I guess a gun would be too much to ask for," he said dryly.

"No gun. No horse. Take it or leave it."

He didn't like his chances. His leg was suspect. On foot and weaponless, against six well-heeled desperadoes who knew the swamp better than he ever would. But he had no alternative. Flicking the spent cigarette away, he got to his feet and gingerly tested his injured leg. It buckled under him. He caught himself against the table, looked around at their faces. No sympathy. Not that he'd expected any. They were afraid of him. He saw that now. Afraid of what he stood for. Their fear permeated the room. They masked it with hate. They were impatient for the five minutes to pass, so that they could destroy what they were afraid of. Gantry smiled grimly. Five minutes and he might manage to make it out the door.

Outside, the hounds started to raise cain.

"Rider coming!" hollered one of the outlaws on the porch.

Mark moved like greased lightning, shoving Gantry roughly as he swung toward the door. Gantry tripped over the split-log bench and hit the floor.

Framed in the doorway, Mark said, "Looks like Doc Treadgold."

"What's he doing here?" wondered Watt.

"Fetch him," said Ma.

Watt and Mark went outside. Gantry crawled up onto the bench. Matt kept a wary eye on him. Like the others, Gantry wondered what had brought Treadgold. Still trying to prevent bloodshed, probably. Gantry wasn't encouraged. Seemed like the more Treadgold tried to mediate, the louder the guns talked. Gantry figured Treadgold had already done the most he could do—a brief stay of execution.

Mark shouted the dogs down. A moment later, Treadgold stepped through the door, carrying his medical grip. He nodded to Gantry.

"Looks like you'd have to get better to die," was his comment.

"Could be worse," said Gantry.

"What brings you, Doc?" asked Ma.

"I said I'd be back to check on Luke, Mrs. Foley."

She cackled. "*Mrs.* Foley! Ain't he a gentleman boys?"

Treadgold laid the grip on the table, opened it, froze at the deadly double-click sound of a revolver being cocked.

"Put that goddamn gun down, Watt!" barked Ma, infuriated.

"Don't trust him," mumbled Watt.

"After all he's done for me and mine, Doc's welcome here," said Ma sternly. "Now you lay that thumb-buster aside, or I'm gonna put about a half-pound of double-ought into your mangy hide."

"No call to talk to your own brother like that," groused Watt. But he lowered the gun.

Treadgold reached into the bag, extracted a vial of white powder.

"I brought you some more quinine in the powder, Mrs. Foley."

"See there, Watt?" asked Ma, simpering. "Doc takes care of me. Don't you, Doc?"

"Yes. I'm going to take care of you."

He uncorked the vial, poured the contents into the jug of corn liquor, carried the jug to her.

"You take it with your whiskey, don't you?" he asked softly.

For a moment his back was turned to the others in the room. Ma Foley laid the LeMat grapeshot pistol aside to accept the jug. Treadgold swung around so that he could watch Watt and the Foley boys, and when he did they saw for the first time the gun in his hand. Gantry recognized it. The .38 Forehand & Wadsworth of Joshua Thorn's. Treadgold had the pistol against Ma Foley's temple.

"Nobody moves," he said. "Matt, call the others in here."

201

Chapter Thirty

Ma Foley ran a gauntlet of strong emotions. Disbelief, sadness, rage. Gantry remembered an old saying: *Hell hath no fury like a woman scorned.* She glanced at the LeMat on the wagon seat next to her.

"Don't," pleaded Treadgold. "I don't want to kill you."

Gantry felt like telling the good doctor that he was going to have to do just that. Treadgold had betrayed Ma Foley's trust. As long as she drew breath, his life wasn't worth a Rebel shinplaster.

"You've made a big mistake, Doc," snarled Mark Foley.

He and his brother and Watt had their hands on the butts of their pistols, but no one had actually drawn his shooting iron out of its holster. Not yet. They were on the verge. Treadgold had made a potentially fatal error, thought Gantry. You didn't put a gun to someone's head and then express your reluctance to use it. Gantry figured it was time he bought in.

Mark was the nearest. Gantry came up off the bench, got behind him before he could turn, and hooked his left arm around Mark's throat. He bent Mark backwards, strangling him, rolling him off the hip. Mark pulled his side gun. Gantry grabbed the pistol with his right hand and twisted it. Mark had to either let go or suffer a broken trigger finger. He let go. Gantry released him, stepped away. Mark hit the floor, rolled, came up on his knees gagging and gasping for air.

Putting his back to the cabin wall, to one side of the door, Gantry aimed the gun at Mark Foley.

"Matt, you've got to the count of three to do as he says. Maybe you don't think he'll shoot. But you better know I will."

Matt didn't hesitate. "Clancy! You and the boys get in here!"

They sauntered in, unprepared for trouble, blissfully unaware of the standoff. The first man through stared at Treadgold and Ma. The second one bumped into the first, saw Gantry off to one side, clawed for the gun in his holster. Gantry hit him across the bridge of the nose with the barrel of Mark's six-gun. He collapsed in a heap. The third man, halfway through the door, turned to make a run for it. Gantry stepped into the doorway, cocked the gun. The man stopped dead in his tracks and reached for the sky. He hadn't made it off the porch.

"You're going the wrong way," snapped Gantry.

Wearing a sullen glower, the man entered the cabin. As he passed by, Gantry plucked the pistol out of his holster.

Nine people were packed into the room—one out

cold on the floor. Too many people, thought Gantry.
Too many guns. It was a situation that could swiftly
spin out of control. He couldn't see everyone's hands.
He and Treadgold, on the face of it, seemed to have
the advantage. But they were opposed by desperate
men who were accustomed to taking desperate
chances. The tide was turning; Gantry could feel it.
They were measuring the odds. He could see it in
their furtive eyes. In a minute, maybe less, someone
would make his play, and the shooting would start.

Horses were tied up outside. Gantry decided it was
just barely possible that he and Treadgold could get
away. It was less likely they could control this room
for very much longer.

Treadgold was thinking along those same lines.

"Go on, Marshal. Get out of here."

Gantry admired the man's bravery. Treadgold was
still utterly committed to saving lives—in this
instance, Gantry's. Now he was manifesting a
willingness to forfeit his own life for his convictions.
He wasn't going to shoot Ma Foley. It was pure bluff.
Gantry realized it, and at that moment, so did Ma.

"You ain't gonna pull that trigger, Doc," she said.
"You ain't got what it takes."

She reached for the grapeshot pistol.

Watt Daggett pushed Matt Foley aside and aimed
his pistol at Gantry.

"Shoot, Doc!" yelled Gantry. He fired as he spoke.

The crashing din of several .44's fired at once filled
the room. Watt's bullet smacked into the door frame
behind Gantry. Gantry's aim was better. Watt spun
and fell. The other men were drawing iron and
diving for what little cover the room's few furnish-

ings provided. Curses, collisions, general confusion. Gantry glanced to the rear of the room. Ma had fired the LeMat point-blank into Treadgold's chest. The doctor staggered and bumped blindly into the table. The Forehand & Wadsworth slipped from his fingers, clattered on the floor. He was looking right at Gantry, but Gantry didn't think he was seeing anything. A quirky smile wrenched at his mouth. Then he stumbled and fell dead.

Gantry backed out of the cabin, blasting away with both pistols. He didn't aim; he didn't think he had to. He sprayed the room with hot lead and knew he was bound to hit something.

As he spun toward the horses, the hounds came at him.

He put two bullets into the nearest. As the second lunged, snarling and spuming, Gantry pulled both triggers again. His heart skipped a beat as both hammers fell on empty chambers. He used the empty gun in his right hand like a club, putting everything he had into the blow. He heard the beast's skull crack. The dog's impetus carried its convulsing body into him, knocking him down. Gantry got up, lurched forward, yanked at the reins of one of the horses tied to the porch uprights. The horse shied away, spooked by the too-close body of one of the hounds, thrashing in its death throes. Gantry clutched at the saddle, hanging on for dear life as the horse took off. He threw his right leg over the cantle, his injured left leg dragging.

A stumbling Watt Daggett was the first man out of the cabin. Gantry's bullet had caught him in the belly. But he was too tough and too mean to die easy.

He fired twice. Gantry felt the horse shudder, stumble. He let go, hit the ground, and rolled. The dying horse took a nosedive.

Bracing himself against a porch upright, Watt drew a bead on Gantry.

Then he saw Mercy.

Her gray gelding was charging out of the swamp, splashing through the shallows. Her yellow hair was streaming. Watt swung the gun in her direction, and hesitated.

Twenty paces from the cabin, she checked the horse. As the gray settled down on its hindquarters, she hurled a bundle of dynamite sticks. The dynamite hit the ground just shy of the porch, then rolled underneath the planking upon which Watt stood. He saw it clearly—three sticks tied together, a long fuse burned all the way down . . .

"Mercy!" he yelled, a cry of pure outrage.

The dynamite exploded.

The blast hurled Watt Daggett's mangled remains ten feet. A horse went down shrieking, mortally wounded in the hail of wood shrapnel. The explosion destroyed half the porch. Burning timbers creaked, cracked, and gave way—part of the roof collapsed in a rending crash. A horse lit out, broken rein leather dangling, and crow-hopped like a bronc. Two more were backstepping, dragging part of a post to which they were still attached.

Mercy reined the gray around, rode to Gantry. She jumped out of the saddle. Gantry was about at the end of his rope. Somehow he got to his feet, lurched like a drunken man. He felt her arm around him, her body against his. He looked deep into her violet eyes,

206

and drew new strength from them.

Coughing and cursing, Matt Foley kicked blackened timbers out of his way as he emerged from the cabin, gray black smoke swirling about him. Mark followed, his right arm dangling uselessly in a blood-soaked sleeve. Spotting Gantry and Mercy through bleary, smoke-stung eyes, they began to shoot.

Mercy held the gelding's reins in one hand—now she gave them to Gantry. He knew what she wanted him to do. Get on the horse. She would get on behind. They would make a run for it. Under the circumstances, flight was the only viable option. He was unarmed, and Mercy didn't appear to be heeled, either.

His left leg was useless; he tried to mount the gray on the "Indian side," right foot in rightside stirrup. The gelding shied away, disconcerted. Gantry muttered an oath, hanging onto the saddle as the horse sidestepped, his injured leg dragging. He managed to crawl into the saddle, neck-reined harshly. The gray calmed and responded. Gantry reached out to Mercy. She reached up to him. He heard the bullet strike. Her fingers brushed his as she slumped against the gelding's girth, the horse danced away, snorting, and Mercy fell.

Gantry yelled. A hoarse, incoherent, guttural sound. Rage mixed with anguish.

Matt and Mark were coming through the smoke, firing steadily. Without second thought, Gantry slid off the gray. His left leg buckled. He stumbled, fell, crawled, reached her. She moved slightly. *Thank God, she moved.* Bullets buzzed like angry hornets, drummed the ground. He covered her body with his own.

The shooting subsided as the Foleys reloaded, and in the lull Gantry heard the hoofbeats of a galloping horse. The crackling report of a long gun was quickly answered by the booming percussion of the Foleys' pistols. Mercy's yellow hair in his eyes, Gantry raised his head to see Joshua Thorn riding out of the swamp. Joshua was trying to wield his Winchester one-handed, the reins in the other. Shooting a rifle one-handed while on a galloping horse was a feat better left to trick-shot artists, so Gantry harbored little hope Joshua would hit anything but a piece of Texas Redlands.

Joshua had one advantage: the Winchester's range. But every second, every stride of his stretched-out horse, shortened the distance between him and the Foleys. He thundered past Gantry and Mercy. A heartbeat later he was somersaulting off the back of his horse. The Winchester sailed through the air. Gantry rolled away from Mercy, spent his last reserve of strength to get to his feet. That rifle was his one and only chance. He broke into a shambling run.

The Foley boys were coming on. Having dealt with Joshua Thorn, they turned their attention and their guns on Gantry. Shooting, reloading. Walking, not running, cocooned in white powder smoke. Knowing—as did Gantry—that the closer they got, the sooner they would win. Outside twenty feet, a man with a side gun had to aim his shots—not always easy for a man under fire.

Diving for the rifle, Gantry rolled, sat up, worked the repeater's lever action. A spent shell casing spun away. How many bullets left? One way to find out. Stock to shoulder, he took careful aim. A bullet plucked at his trouser leg. He'd survived too many gunfights to panic. He refused to rush his shot. Cool and steady, he squeezed the trigger. The Winchester kicked. He saw the puff of dust off Matt's shirt as the bullet punched the oldest Foley brother dead-center.

Mark yelled as he saw his brother fall. He emptied his pistol. Gantry was hit as he levered another round into the Winchester's breech. A numbing impact, a tingling sensation, then a fast-spreading cold, a copperish taste in his mouth. Mark was running toward him, dropping the empty six-gun, brandishing a knife. The blade flashed in brittle morning sunlight sifting through the cypress. Gantry fired. Again his aim was true. Mark stumbled, sprawled, lay still.

Letting the Winchester slip from his grasp, Gantry tried one more time to get up. Just one more time. All he could think about was Mercy. He couldn't make it. No strength left. Resigned, he lay on his back and stared at the sky, astonished by a loud silence. All he could hear was his pulse. He listened to it slowing gradually. His eyelids were heavy. He was so very, very tired. With a curious detachment, he accepted the fact he was dying.

He lost track of time, drifted in and out of consciousness. Two gunshots startled him. His eyes snapped open. He looked up into the big, red, square face of a grim Bull Tennally.

"Is he dead?"

Logan's voice.

"Not yet," replied Bull.

Logan hove into view.

"Mercy," said Gantry.

209

Bull frowned, glanced at Logan. "He's tryin' to say something."

Again Gantry spoke her name.

Logan sighed. He looked bitter.

"Yeah," he said, "she'll make it. Will you?"

Gantry smiled.

Chapter Thirty-One

Three weeks later, Joshua Thorn and his wife came calling at Hannah Malone's house. Gantry was sitting in a rocker on the front gallery. He was smoking a cigarette, watching storm clouds gather. A warm spring breeze was redolent with the fragrance of wildflowers, heavy with the scent of rain.

Laura Thorn was driving the buggy. She had a little trouble with the balky mule in the traces, as she brought the buggy to a stop at the foot of the gallery steps.

"I'm still learning," she admitted to Gantry, a touch defensive. "There are so many things a woman must learn to do out here. Things she'd never ever be called upon to do back East."

"Looks like you're a quick learner," replied Gantry.

She placed her hand on Joshua's. "I'm trying."

Securing the harness around the buggy stock, she got out and gave her husband a helping hand. Joshua was embarrassed that he needed help.

Bandaging bulked his right trouser leg. His left arm was in a cast and sling. Foley bullets had struck him in both arm and leg, in the first instance breaking the bone. He looked pale and sweaty, his cheeks hollowed, dark blotches under his eyes. The ride out had cost him.

Relying on a hickory cane with a staghorn handle, he hobbled up the steps, Laura providing additional support.

"Hell, Laura," he groused. "You don't have to baby me."

"I will if I want to. And I'll thank you to start watching your language." A sweet glowing smile took the sting out of the scolding. "We're going to have a son soon, and I don't want him picking up bad habits from his father. I declare, you Texans are a crude and profane lot."

Hannah Malone came through the open front door in time to hear Laura's harangue. She wiped flour-dusted hands on her apron, brushed an errant strand of iron gray hair from her eyes.

"So it's going to be a boy child, is it?"

"She's decided," said Joshua wryly, easing into a chair next to Gantry's with a sigh of vast relief. Gantry's shirt was open, and Joshua could see the dressing wrapped tightly around the lawman's chest. "Well, don't we make a fine pair," he laughed. "How do you feel?"

"Only hurts when I breathe."

"Mercy?"

Gantry nodded.

"May I see her?" Laura asked the widow woman.

Hannah nodded, then glanced at Gantry.

"Have you seen Willie, Marshal?"

"No, ma'am."

Striving to mask her concern, Hannah took Laura inside.

"Looks like rain," remarked Joshua.

"Yep."

"That Cajun doc up from San Augustine—what do you think of him?"

"He'll do."

"I suppose he knows his business. But I can't understand half of what he says." Joshua gazed bleakly across neglected fields at a line of wind-thrashed pines. "I must confess I . . . miss Doctor Treadgold."

"He was a good man."

"I can't help but blame myself. I didn't want to let him go in alone. But he insisted. Said it was the only way to get you out."

They lapsed into moody silence.

A few minutes later, Joshua said, "I'm delighted to hear Mercy will pull through."

Gantry didn't respond. His feelings ran too deep and strong on the subject to put into words.

Misreading Gantry's reticence, Joshua's temper slow-burned.

"You could do a lot worse. She was ready to die for you."

"Been too much dying."

"When you came out of the Foley cabin, she lit that dynamite and took off before I could stop her. It was her idea to swing by the Daggett place and get that stuff. She's the one led the Doc and me through the Big Cypress."

Again, Gantry did not reply. Joshua tapped the gallery planking with the copper tip of his walking stick.

213

"There are other lines of work, Marshal."

"You told me that once before."

"Bears repeating."

"It's all I've known."

"A hell of a job. Shooting people, or getting shot. Me, I'm going to hang my shingle in Tenaha and practice law. Now that there's going to *be* some law in Shelby County."

Hannah Malone returned to the gallery, walked to the end of it, and watched the northern approach of the Trammel Trace.

"What is it, ma'am?" asked Joshua.

"Rider coming."

The first drops of rain splattered on the gallery roof. By the time the horseman reached the house, it was coming down in wind-lashed sheets. The man sloshed up onto the gallery, tipped the dripping brim of an old campaign hat to Hannah Malone. A leather-skinned, squinty-eyed, bandy-legged character, with big blunt hands and rugged unshaven features.

"Howdy, ma'am."

Hannah was watchful, reserved. "Howdy."

The man unbuttoned his yellow slicker, and they saw the ball-pointed badge pinned to his shirt.

"Buck Stonecipher's my handle. United States Marshal."

"Hannah Malone. Forgive my poor manners. It's just that I've seen a lot of trouble come down that road."

"So I hear."

"Step inside and dry off by the stove, Marshal. I'll pour you a cup of coffee."

"That'll suit me right down to the ground, ma'am.

214

But first I'd like to palaver with Mr. Gantry here."

Joshua Thorn climbed gingerly out of the chair and, with a polite nod at Stonecipher, limped inside. Hannah followed him. Stonecipher slacked into the vacated chair. Gantry watched the slanting rain pummel his boots and soak his trousers from the knees down.

"Real fence-lifter," observed Stonecipher.

"Rains a lot in these parts."

"You did good work, Jim. Clearing out the Foley gang took some doing. You look like warmed-over hell. I just moseyed over to see how you were faring."

Gantry smiled. Stonecipher had "moseyed" almost three hundred miles.

"I reckon you've come to try and talk me out of it."

Stonecipher tipped his hat back, dug a crumpled telegram out of his damp shirt pocket. He smoothed the paper out on his leg and read it for the thousandth time.

"Never figured you'd quit, Jim. You were born to tote a badge."

"Tenaha needs a sheriff."

"This ain't your kind of country."

"I'm getting used to it."

Gantry held out his hand. Stonecipher stared morosely at the badge.

"So you're finished."

"Nope. Just getting started."

"Hate to lose a good man."

"There are plenty more."

"Not enough."

"Sometimes you have to look twice before you see them."

Stonecipher wasn't one to give up without a fight.

"Dammit, Jim. Likely gonna be pretty tame around here from now on. You might get bored."

"Good. I'll put down roots. Raise a family. Live to be an old man. Do something with my life."

Stonecipher peered at him skeptically.

"Kid Spence is dead," said Gantry, soft and low. "I've been wasting my time. Hunting down a dead man for twenty years. I was doing the right thing for the wrong reasons."

"Nothing wrong with revenge."

"Yes, there is. I've seen that here. The Foleys and the Thorns have been killing each other for forty years, and what good's come of it? Blood for blood doesn't work, Buck."

Stonecipher took the badge out of Gantry's hand. Slow and stiff, he stood up, looked askance at the woods and the rain.

"Better learn to swim, amigo. Feller could drown in these parts."

Gantry laughed, relieved that Stonecipher appeared willing to accept his decision with good grace.

"Reckon I'll go sample some of that Mrs. Malone's java. Wait for this frog-strangler to pass before I move on. Can't hardly wait to get back on dry land, hoss. Where you can see farther than you could ride on a long day. 'Course, I'd be obliged was you to introduce me to the little lady."

"What?"

"Well, I ain't stone blind. Appears you've got something to live for. Nine times out of ten, that something wears a dress."

"Sometimes she does," grinned Gantry.

Chapter Thirty-Two

As was her custom, Hannah Malone woke with the dawn. Yesterday's storm had passed. The sky was robin egg blue, the color of her eyes. She pulled iron gray hair back and bound it into a tight bun, washed her face with water from the blue enamel bowl on the dresser. When the cock crowed she was down the hall, tapping hopefully on Willie's door. Tapping, tapping . . . but no sound from within. She opened the door, her heart plummeting, and saw that his bed had not been slept in. The third night in a row.

Sick with despair, afraid Willie was gone for good, she went downstairs to the kitchen. Gantry had stocked the iron stove with kindling last night. She got a fire going, water in the coffeepot, the coffeepot on the stove. Wood was stacked in the stone hearth—Gantry again. He had replenished the woodpile, repaired the porch rail broken weeks earlier in his donnybrook with Joshua Thorn, done other things around the house that had long needed attention. She'd tried to dissuade him, but he kept on. Doggedly building up his strength, testing his quick-to-mend body.

She looked bleakly around the kitchen, listless and depressed. She needed to get breakfast started. The Thorns and Buck Stonecipher had not stayed over, but Gantry and Mercy were still her guests—had been since Logan had left them in her keeping.

But she just didn't feel like doing anything. For years she'd lived with the fear that one day, out of the blue, Willie might pick up and leave. Tried to prepare herself for the day. Now she realized there was really no way to prepare for being left utterly alone, with no one to do for. Everyone needed somebody. Folks who only did for themselves lived empty lives.

Boot heels thumped on the stairs. While she knew it was Gantry, she couldn't help but pray that by some miracle, it would be Willie appearing in the doorway.

"Morning, ma'am."

"Good morning, Marshal."

Her civility was strained. Gantry could tell, and he knew the reason. He felt sorry for her, wanted to tell her so, and thought better of it. Sympathy was sometimes too cruel.

"I'll go fetch the eggs," he offered.

"No, Marshal. I will. You sit yourself down."

"I'm not a marshal any more, Mrs. Malone," he reminded, her smiling.

She forced herself to return the smile, stepped out the back door, and saw Willie standing at the foot of the steps. Her hand flew to her throat; the sight wrenched a gasp from her.

"Willie! What's happened to you? Are you all right?"

His clothes were filthy and torn. He looked like he hadn't eaten or slept for days. Eyes sunk deep in their sockets stared feverishly out of a face smudged with grime. He didn't seem to recognize her.

"Where have you been, Willie?"

"Around," was his sullen reply.

"I was worried sick," said Hannah.

"Don't need to worry about me. I can take care of myself."

Gantry appeared in the doorway behind Hannah. There was nothing friendly in the way Willie looked at him.

"I worry, all the same," said Hannah. "You're like a son to me, Willie. You know that. I love you as much as I did my own flesh and blood."

"I'm not your son. Don't want to be. I want to be somebody. Somebody else . . ."

"Somebody like Luke Foley, maybe," said Gantry.

"Luke Foley wasn't so bad."

Hero worship, thought Gantry. Too often, young men unhappy with their lot sought to follow in the footsteps of men like Luke Foley. Young men who were tired of doing without, and wanting to trade drudgery for excitement. Luke Foley and those like him, men who took what they wanted and led lives of adventure, became role models.

"You'd better go inside and get cleaned up," said Hannah. "Breakfast will be ready soon."

Willie brushed rudely past them. Crestfallen, Hannah watched him go.

"He was an orphan," she told Gantry. "I took him

in after the war. Tried to do right by him."

"I'm sure you have."

"At least he came back. That means something, doesn't it?"

She did not sound too convinced, and when she turned away to cross the yard, the weight of dejection sloped her shoulders.

Logan Thorn dropped by in time for breakfast.

Hannah did not much care for the notorious elder Thorn, but she did a creditable job of masking her feelings, and invited him to sit at table. She made it clear that guns were not permitted in her dining room. Logan hung his pair of .44 Remingtons on a rack in the hallway.

He sat next to Willie, across from Gantry and Mercy. He didn't touch his food. Devoted most of his attention to Mercy.

"You ain't wearing the dress I gave you," he said.

"It's covered with blood," she replied. "Mrs. Malone was kind enough to give me this one."

"Had to take it up quite a bit," said Hannah, at the end of the table. "Poor child's thin as a rail."

"The bullet passed clean through your side," said Logan. "You lost a lot of blood. I'm glad I got there when I did."

"Yes," said Gantry, aggravated. "You saved her life. Thanks."

Logan's lopsided smile was not really a smile at all.

"Don't mention it. By the way, I found something else besides your badge and the Henry." Logan took the clasp knife from his shirt pocket. He slid it across the table. Gantry picked it up. "Figured it must be yours, with those initials carved in the grips."

"My father's," said Gantry.

"Forgot to leave it here. Wanted to get it to you before you left."

"Sorry, Logan. I've got bad news. I'm not going anywhere."

"That's not bad news. If you're staying, it means Mercy's staying, too."

"Mercy and I are going to be married, Logan."

He hadn't asked her. She looked at him now, her violet eyes wide with astonishment. Gantry was annoyed with himself, knowing there were more appropriate ways to ask a woman for her hand in marriage, realizing he was staking a claim, warning Logan off. He'd never been jealous before, and he didn't know how to handle himself.

"That so, Mercy?" asked Logan.

"Yes. That's so." She sounded out of breath.

Logan drummed his fingers on the table top. He was slacked in his chair, but the casual pose was a facade. Strong and dangerous emotions provoked him.

It was obvious to Gantry that he and Logan were headed for a collision. Too much bad blood between them. It would happen sooner or later. This was as good a time as any. Gantry pushed the issue.

"You killed Luke, didn't you, Logan?"

Logan's pale blue eyes were hooded.

"What if I did? You did for Matt and Mark and the old she-wolf herself. Joshua tells me you came out of the cabin blasting away. That must've been when Ma

221

Foley got hers. Best piece of work you ever did."

"Foley or not, she was dead-set on giving me a fair chance. Which is more than you gave Rike Bartell in the Buckskin Saloon."

Logan laughed softly. "You're still singing that song?"

"Did Luke get a fair chance, Logan? Or did you shoot him down in cold blood, like you did Bartell? I heard two shots. I bet they were both yours. One for the man out cold just inside the cabin door, and one for Luke, laid up in the back room. 'Cause there were no survivors, were there? I'm curious. Was Luke even conscious when you killed him?"

"He got what he deserved," said Logan, his tone flat and deadly. He finished off his coffee, glanced at Hannah. "Mind if I get some more crank, ma'am?"

"I'll fetch it," said Willie, scraping his chair back, going into the kitchen.

"You act like you're better than the Foleys," said Gantry. "But I don't see two-bits worth of difference between you."

"Fine way to talk about the man who saved your bacon."

"You didn't do that for my sake."

"So what are you going to do about it?"

"I don't have to do anything but wait. The Foleys and Daggetts are dead. You can't use the feud for an excuse. But you're still full of hate, and you'll keep killing. I think you've got a notion about killing me."

"You have to take what you want in this world," said Logan.

Willie reappeared with the coffeepot. He filled

Logan's cup. Logan was staring at Mercy again, and paid Willie no attention. Willie was the kind of person others tended to overlook. Gantry didn't pay him any mind, either, until he saw the gun in Willie's hand.

"Willie, no!"

Willie fired point-blank into the back of Logan's head.

Gantry felt the warm spray of blood on his face as Logan's upper body hammered the table hard enough to splinter the wood.

"That's for Luke Foley, you bastard!" screamed Willie.

He dropped the coffeepot and bolted for the hallway. Kicking back his chair, Gantry rose, took two strides in pursuit, only to pull up short as Willie whirled and menaced him with the pistol. Smoke curled from the barrel aimed at Gantry's chest.

"Don't come after me, mister!"

"Think you're somebody now, don't you?"

"I am!" cried Willie. "I'm the man who killed Logan Thorn." He backed into the hallway, then made a dash for the front door.

Gantry went after him.

Willie had snatched Logan's gun belt off the rack on his way out. Gantry saw his Henry repeater leaning in a corner, fetched it. Willie bounded off the gallery and onto Logan's horse. As Gantry came out of the house, Willie kicked the horse into a gallop, across the yard, beneath the elms clothed in new green, making for the Trammel Trace.

Gantry put the Henry to his shoulder and drew a bead on the fleeing man.

Then he lowered the rifle.

Just another Kid Spence, he thought. He didn't have to kill Willie. Willie had killed himself the second he'd pulled the trigger.

He turned to face Hannah, standing in the doorway, tears streaming down a face etched deep by the years of hardship and tragedy.

She watched Willie ride away, the hooves of his stretched-out horse kicking up clods of red mud as he escaped down the road to hell.

Slipping by her, Gantry confronted Mercy in the hall.

"You goin' after him?" she asked.

"No," he said, and as she stepped closer, he dropped the rifle and put his arms around her. She turned her face up, and he brushed yellow hair out of her violet eyes, kissed her small round mouth with its hairline scar at the corner.

"I'm beginning to like it around here . . ."